Turn That Floozie

"A,"

Thank you for supporting
my dream. I hope you love
it! May you & your family
live a long life of love &
happiness

[handwritten signature]

Turn That Floozie

Ilaya Delaney

Library of Congress Control Number:		2010908198
ISBN:	Hardcover	978-1-4500-9264-7
	Softcover	978-1-4500-9263-0
	Ebook	978-1-4500-9265-4

This book was printed in the United States of America.

To order additional copies of this book, contact:
Xlibris Corporation
1-888-795-4274
www.Xlibris.com
Orders@Xlibris.com
77527

Acknowledgments

I would like to thank my parents who love me unconditionally, my best friend who put up with me, and my pastor and his wife for guiding me.

Chapter One

Looking over her shoulder, Natasha Billingsworth caught a glance of Bruce Wilson correcting his tie in the wall-mounted cherrywood frame mirror. One quick glance in her compact revealed an unattractive smudge of kissable gloss by Chanel. Natasha counted sleeping with the boss as a cost of doing business.

Sitting on the mahogany desk, Natasha fastened the last button of her Tahari suit with the satisfaction of having the feeling of control. The money was just inkling to the reason she did what she did; getting paid for it was just a bonus.

"Mr. Wilson, your wife is on line one," says Ashley Brooke, Bruce's assistant for the past two years. Bruce hurries to the phone as he returns his blazer to his middle-aged shoulders.

"Hunny, how was your day, and are you set for the party tonight?"

Looking at the forced smile on Bruce's face made Natasha feel a little guilty for what she had just done. As quickly as this feeling fell on her, it vanished when he signed over twelve one-thousand-dollar money orders to Natasha. She mouthed, "You're welcome" and exited the room, closing the door gently so all that one could hear was the clicking of the lock.

It is the beginning of a long weekend for Natasha. The company party is tonight to celebrate a big quarter for the company. She is disgusted with the thought of having to smile at the people she hates and dodges Bruce's wife, so she will not have to make meaningless small talk. Although the music of the money-counting machines is blaring in her ears when she glances at Bruce or his wife Mourna gives her comfort and an instant smirk like a chess player who has full sight of their victory.

The ringing of Natasha's cell phone interrupts her cheeriness. Checking her caller ID, an abrupt sense of irritation floods every unction of her being.

"Mom, this must be important because you never call me at this hour and on my cell."

"Girl, 'hay, how're you' is the way you greet a person whether you know them or not, Nat," Michelle said with a sigh.

On the outward appearance, no one could tell she was from Mississippi, but when she opens her mouth, the accent is permanent in the memory of those who converse with her. "I do call . . . you just never answer or return my calls. I have to get your father to call, just to see how you're doin'. I did not raise you to be antisociable, especially to me. *I am your mother.*"

"How could I possibly forget?"

"Are you still coming for Sunday brunch?"

"I completely forgot . . . I told Landry I would go to the debut of her clothing line."

"It's just brunch. You would think y'all had to rearrange your existence. It is at eleven thirty, and we should be done eating in an hour. We haven't seen you in years and years, longer than that for Landry since Melvin passed. I know, why don't you both come?"

"Okay, Ma, I will ask Landry and call you tonight. I am on my way to Nerge now."

"Well, if you are on your way, I can stay on the line until you get together because I know you forget."

"It is not that serious. I will call you tonight. Good-bye."

Even after she hung up the phone, Natasha had mixed emotions. Michelle Green Billingsworth might be married and a mom, but her past actions say she is far from a wife and a mother. The only occupation she had prior to her marriage was at *My Ladies,* a local strip club, where her stage name was "Fantasy," and she worked the hardest for the high rollers who came in on Fridays to unwind from the workweek. Michelle knew all too well about a hard not life. She was a time-stopping beauty in her day. Bryant Billingsworth, the president of a product development firm, just happened to be the catch that she managed to get to settle down and marry her. He was in town for only a few days before she hypnotized him with her irresistible charm to the point where he couldn't live without her. Before you knew it, he sent her a car and paid for frequent flights to New York. By the second trip, Bryant popped the question. Of course, she said yes. Snagging Bryant brought the bank account she always dreamed of. She couldn't leave her brother Melvin behind, though. Michelle transferred ten thousand dollars a month to her brother so that he could move to the *Big Apple* and start over as she did. Michelle didn't mind pretending to love Bryant and keeping the house in order. She had taken care of her younger brother with little to no income except what she brought in from the club and what money he brought in working in the mill and cropping the field. Her dreams of royal living were big enough for both of them.

Chapter Two

Natasha entered Nerge with the same head-turning captivation Michelle mastered in her prime. A certain onlooker, who once was assured that there wasn't a decent woman in New York City, couldn't take his eyes away, staring at her polished pedicure feet seductively entrapped in a pair of stilettos, which heightened her stature and added more definition to her sculpted legs. She was dressed in business attire, the classic short dress with a long jacket. Her hair illuminated from the reflection of the sun. Those auburn strands danced around her beautiful face as the wind disagreed with the door's opening. Breathtaking and beautiful was this bronze goddess in the eyes of Jeffrey Pattman. This was defiantly a perk seeing how he discovered the vice president was laundering money from the company whom he is always on the defense.

Natasha stopped by the bar of this down-home, soulful eatery with its city coffeehouse interior. She met Landry's eyes as she scanned the room for her location but not before the intense look lock that she and Jeffrey held with such gravitational force it took all she had to pull her eyes away and focus. This sudden urge Natasha never experienced with anyone of her boy toys. It shook her down to her bones with the fear that for one moment, she wasn't in control.

Landry is your classic natural beauty. She has sandy blonde curly hair that is never tamed. Her eclectic wardrobe depicts her creativity as a designer. Landry's light hazel eyes and fair complexion always left minds wondering if she was really Melvin's child. Michelle didn't make it easy for Landry and Melvin Jr.'s mother, the late Selena Green. There was a rough patch in the marriage around the time Landry would have been conceived. A little encouragement from Michelle only made it harder for Melvin to accept Landry as his child. The blood test proved that he was the father, but the whole situation made their relationship icy.

"Greetings, Nat," proclaimed Landry as she embraced her closest kin. "Oooooh, you got that look about you again. When are you going to . . . never mind."

"Thank you. Last I checked, you didn't refuse the money to start your clothing line," said Natasha with a cocked neck and flared nostrils. It killed Natasha knowing that Landry could read her like a book and didn't mind voicing her perceptions.

"That was before I knew the primary lender. We are not going to do this right now. I am sorry I said anything about the sinful glow you have about you. Did you receive your ticket to the show?"

"Did. I am surprised I am the only one you dot a ticket for. What about your friend Rob? Has it gone cold already?"

Landry gave a deep eye roll of disgust. "He was the reason Google became so popular. Every word that came out of his mouth was a lie. Rob told me he was a surgeon . . . the brother was an orderly at that hospital. He said he had no children . . . boy had seventeen with fifteen different women. I was afraid of going out into public with him because there may be a mob of children screaming 'Daddy, Daddy, Daddy.' The bad thing about it is that I met him at church. Liars have their place in the hellfire."

"I do not attend for that reason. Most of the people who attend are just pretending and scouting for victims, too much drama!"

"Nat, some people go to church to actually get their problems worked out and to find God."

"I do not need to know him. I am just fine. How come every time I eat with you, we end up talking about God? You know how I feel about that."

Inhaling deep, Landry began to say proudly, "He is a part of me internally. If He is in you He is bound to come out, especially in conversation."

"Subject change! My mom wants us to come to Sunday brunch at the house. She wants us there by eleven thirty." In her mind, Natasha was hoping Landry would say she had to be at the tent early for the show so that she could act out. The fantasy of her lying between her Egyptian cotton sheets was soon burst.

"Sounds good to me, I could use some home cooking. Wait, who's cooking, if I recall correctly your mother hasn't cooked in years." Landry's expression shows pure concern.

Natasha was staring out of the wide windows of the restaurant, her mind obviously not on the conversation.

She could act out the fantasy of her lying between her Egyptian cotton sheets, but the fantasy bubble was burst. A snap of the fingers from Landry brought her back to the conversation, "Earth to Nat, what's up with you?"

Natasha's face was so serious that Landry was afraid to say another word. "Dry Greens, I haven't been to that house in years. I have no idea why Mom is insisting on my visiting. What makes this Sunday or any other day different from the rest." Dry Greens is the nickname Natasha gave Landry when they were girls. Somehow Natasha put together the last three letters of Landry's name and her favorite southern dish at the age of seven. It took no time for it to grow on Landry.

There are certain precautions that must be taken when one has a child. Michelle ignored them when Bryant was away on business. She had free reign to do what she wanted. Michelle drowned herself in alcohol and the closest warm body she could find. A housewife should have an eye out for those who enter and exit the premises and how often.

The girls always spent their Friday rush hour in Nerge. Since it was distinctly placed between Natasha's office and Landry's studio, there was no reason they couldn't make time and meet in the middle. Nerge is owned by Melvin Green Jr., Landry's elder brother. He kept in touch with his southern roots when it came to the kitchen and his women. Melvin had a wife and established a restaurant by the age of twenty-five. For his twenty-seventh birthday, it was included as a grand opening party for two more restaurants in the metro area. He married young to sweet RosaLee. A Georgia Peach, who was the most pleasant and humble young lady any man would be proud to have on his arm. It was a great devastation to find out seven years after their marriage that RosaLee would die due to breast cancer. Three years has gone by, and Melvin does not feel it robbery at all because he made a vow and though things were hard, his wife kept her same angelic ways until the end.

"Hey now, what do I owe the pleasure?" said Melvin Jr. with exaggerated enthusiasm.

Landry propped her elbow on the table and placed her chin in her hand giving Melvin a big smile and sarcastic remark, "Like you don't know, we come here often and are great tippers!"

Melvin cocked his brow and darted, "Big tips are great if you pay for the food as well."

"Ha, ha, ha," said Landry as she flung her hand in a "whatever" gesture.

"It's not like I came to talk to you anyway, fat hair." Melvin focused his eyes on Natasha and asked, "How is it going, Nat?"

Landry's mouth shot open with surprise. Natasha started talking before she could make any clever comeback. "All is well in my world. What about yours?"

Melvin pulled a chair from the adjacent table, swung his leg over it, and flopped down with his hands gripping the back and his chest compressed to his knuckles. Melvin was a looker with one blaring unibrow only RosaLee could look past. Melvin makes the tall, dark, and handsome man, with his dark chocolate complexion and being six feet four inches in height. His strong stature is strong enough to make any woman feel secure in his embrace. Yet he is single and not looking. Melvin invests all his time in his restaurants to the point where there is no free time for him to think about his late wife.

Melvin takes a look over his right shoulder to see if Jeffrey was still sitting at the bar. "I never ever play matchmaker, but in this case, I must help the fellow. Do you see the guy at the bar and please don't look at one time like amateurs."

"Yes, and he is a cutie in that Hugo Boss suit," whispered Landry as she leaned across the table toward Natasha.

Natasha did not have to look. An instant memory of the hazel eyes that made time stop in her world sent a burning in her chest that made it hard for her to breathe. Her face became flushed and the feeling of her clammy hands forced her to rub them on her dress. "What is wrong with me? He is only a man," she proclaimed to herself.

"Girl, look . . . what's wrong?" Landry asked her cousin with concern.

"Nothing, nothing, what about him, Melvin?" Natasha asked with a straight face and stern voice.

"He keeps sneaking glances every chance he gets. He's cool. He comes on Fridays when it's rough at work. He's a corporate lawyer for one of these huge corporations nearby, and he is single. You would be surprised what people tell you when they have vodka straight without chaser. Next thing you know I will have my own dating service. I need a life," said Melvin in one breath.

"I couldn't agree with you more, big brother," Landry blurted with a sarcastic smile, then added, "Brother, do not worry about me. He is not my type."

"Huh, your type doesn't discriminate against a wet mop, and I wasn't referring to you anyway."

All eyes turned to Natasha making it hard for her to swallow. She thought the glance that was held between her and the stranger will be her little secret. She didn't want the world to know that the untamable allowed one look to question all that she knows. "What are you looking at me for? I do not approach any man. If he wants me, he must make the

effort to . . ." She didn't hear the footsteps approaching while she was
stating her truth. She noticed a change in everyone's face and was afraid
to say anything further. "What?" she asked.

Jeffrey couldn't believe his feet started to move. He thought in his
mind that he could start up a conversation with Melvin about anything
and hope he would be inclined to introduce him to the purpose of his
greeting. "Be cool, your breath does not stink, and you are not sweating.
Good, Melvin saw you. Hopefully he will stand . . ."

Melvin smiles at Jeffrey pretending he doesn't see his motive, "Yo,
what's up, Jeff," he says standing and putting his hand out. Jeffrey accepts
his hand and asks, "How's business? The pizza was delicious."

"The new restaurant opens in a month, and I can't wait. How are
things at the office?" Melvin says with enthusiasm.

"That's great man. I just found out the VP was embezzling and
accepting bribes so I will be knee-deep in files for the next two months,"
Jeffrey exhaled with exhaustion on his face.

Melvin being a guy got the hint. "Let me not be rude any longer.
Jeffrey, this is my sister Landry and my cousin Natasha. Landry is a
fashion designer whose first show is on Sunday, and Natasha is a senior
marketing executive at Peagles."

Jeffrey smiled and shook Landry's hand first with a friendly nod,
"Nice to meet you," and turned to Natasha to shake her hand to find
that she wasn't looking at him, and she had her hands in her lap under
the table. "Okay," Jeffrey said with a raised brow. He wasn't giving up
just yet. The connection he felt when their eyes met had to be mutual.
She is an extraordinarily attractive woman who must get advances all the
time. He knows she felt it too; otherwise she would conduct herself in
an introduction with the same elegance as she did when she entered the
restaurant. Jeffrey takes a second to regroup and see if he could think of
another entry.

Melvin was disappointed with Natasha's behavior. He pushed his
chair back under the adjacent table and proceeded back to the kitchen.
"I will see you on Sunday, sis," Melvin said as he proceeded to turn and
walk away.

Just then Jeffrey's memory darted back like a bolt of lightning. "Are
your designs couture?"

The question threw everything off guard and raised questions in
Melvin's mind about Jeffrey's sexual orientation. Landry gave Natasha a
foot nudge and answered, "Ready to wear mostly. The couture line will
not be available until fall of next year. Hey, why don't you bring your
boyfriend to the show on Sunday? I think there is room for two more."

A thunderous roar of laughter erupted out of Jeffrey's mouth after Landry's last statement. "If I didn't just meet you I would have been a little offended. That was cute the way you asked to see if I was gay. I am not gay nor am I seeing anyone so there will only be need for one ticket. Thank you for inviting me."

Landry shrugged, "No problem. I am learning to ease my blunt personality by trying to make difficult questions as pretty as possible."

"Your effort didn't go unnoticed."

A clashing of dishes was the sound of money going down the drain. Melvin was hoping for only broken dishes. "Duty calls see ya ladies and men." Melvin shook Jeffrey's hand and rushed to the kitchen.

"Well, ladies, it was nice to meet you both." Jeffrey reached out his hand to Landry giving her hand a firm shake and then turned to Natasha. He saw in Landry's attempt to ask his orientation Natasha became interested in the conversation, and he noticed her looking at him in his peripheral vision. He turned and reached out for Natasha's hand once again with the desire that she would reach for him and take his hand. To his surprise, she obliged by shaking his hand which surprised Jeffrey to see that he wasn't once again rejected, and he rejoiced internally. The radiance of her face was burned into his long-term memory. He could see the sun reflecting in her brown eyes. The way her mouth parted when he grabbed her soft hands made him want to hear everything that would precede her lips. He knew then he could love her. "Are you coming to the fashion show," he asked with her hand still in his.

"I-I will be there."

"Great, I will see you Sunday."

Chapter Three

A sudden feeling of exhaustion came over Natasha as she realized it was six forty-five on the wall-mounted timepiece in the living room. She thought that after a long bath, she would feel better, but it proved to be a failed remedy. The only thing she could think about was the party. Parties and any other gatherings the company has are mandatory for her to attend. Being the Exec over the marketing department has its perks. Natasha gets two hundred eighty hours paid vacation, benefits that pay up to 90 percent with no out-of-pocket expenses, a company car, travel accommodations, and a seven figure salary. Since she's been sleeping with Bruce for the past three years, anything else she wants is given under the table. Natasha loved the feeling of control she had over Bruce. She knew he couldn't resist her, and he would go beyond limits to keep her happy, especially, since he has told her all his dirty secrets about offshore accounts and a multitude of children he has scattered abroad. There was no need for her to do the things she does, but it was like she couldn't help herself.

Natasha has interruptions in her thoughts since the introduction of Jeffrey this afternoon. Landry wouldn't shut up about her reaction and facial expressions while in his presence. There was something about him that intimidated Natasha. This made her feel very uncomfortable. Never has a man put a spell on her, so hypnotizing. Never has a man left her speechless. Never has a man made it hard for her to breathe. Natasha felt as if she were at Jeffrey's mercy. She was not the puppet master in the orchestration of the introduction. This time she met a real man whom she knew would never be held by her strings. The recap of events was interrupted by the blaring sound of the telephone.

"Hello," said Natasha, then checking the caller ID.

It pleased her that the voice on the other end was of the pleasant and faithful tone that she had grown accustomed to over the past five years. Janet Romona, dancer, songwriter, and performer, who Natasha had met at a mixer in Soho. Janet is one who's hard to keep up with. Her music is popular in South America and Spain. She's working on breaking through in the States within the year, which has doubled her workload and tours.

"Stranger, I should be upset that you haven't called or e-mailed me. I was only out of the country, not dead, chica!"

"I would need to call your agents' agent just to leave a message with your assistant. It is great to hear from your sarcastic behind. How are things?"

"Excellent! The shows are selling out, and my family is in good health. If only I could find a decent man who didn't mind my line of work, it would be more perfect. Jesus loves me so it is *all* good."

"I am glad everything is well with you. I am on my way to the company party and . . ."

"Are you still sleeping with the big man? That's going to be awkward if his wife is there. Why are you still sleeping with the guy anyway?"

"Look, I do what I do, and it works for me. Did you call me to give me the third degree?"

"Watch the attitude. Thou shall not commit adultery. That is the word of God, and it seems everyone you hang out with knows that, but you, or you just don't want to know. This thing is going to leave you in a world of hurt. I don't care how good the money is, that you don't need if you haven't noticed!"

"This is the second time today. I am in control of my life. I say and do, and that is all there is to it."

"That may be correct right now, but you will still have to answer to G-O-D!"

"Is there another point that you wanted to make? Otherwise I am hanging up."

"I will be home for a week next month the sixth through the thirteenth, and I was hoping we could vacate. Me calling now should give you enough time to request the vacation since you have to pass it by your bedmate or desk-mate, whatever you guys do it on."

"Funny, I will put it in and e-mail you the confirmation . . ."

"We are just concerned about you, Tasha. If we didn't care, we wouldn't say anything."

"Good-bye, I love you."

"You too chica, love you."

When Natasha placed the receiver on the base, the feeling of guilt that she was trying to conceal surfaced. Her breath became shallow and her heart beat out of control. She sat down on the edge of the bed and placed her head between her legs. A few minutes passed before her breathing became regular again. In the stillness of the room, a still small voice rang in her ears and pierced her conscience saying, "My Word says, 'Thou shall not commit adultery.'" Alarmed and frightened, Natasha rose to her feet and checked her apartment to see if anyone was in her apartment. She looked at her wall-mounted clock, which reflected six twenty-two. Natasha rubbed her hands through her damp hair and released a sigh that brought her to the realization she was holding her breath. The sound of her buzzing doorbell disrupted her feeling of comfort. *Funny, how such a familiar sound can bring discomfort given the situation,* Natasha thought.

"Who is it?" After asking the question, it came back to Natasha's remembrance that Felicia Martin, college bud and best friend, was going to be her date for this event.

"Girl, you're expecting someone else?" asked Felicia with an annoyed tone.

"Come on, up." Natasha unlocked the door and began to toss her untamed hair with not one clue as to what she was to do with it. She bit her lip with frustration as she stared at the mirror over her large leather sectional. Felicia burst through the door with her stilettos in hand and an attitude on her face.

"Great to see you! Do you know that Mr. Martin is going to be out of town for two months," announced Felicia.

"Why do you call your husband, Mr. Martin? What's with the conniption? I am sure your brother, who is a doctor, can make one of his interns write you a fake note so that you can take a few days off and fly out to see him."

"Ahhhh," Felicia sang as she walked across the room toward Natasha with open arms. "You might have saved our marriage. Too bad, we are going to attend the party of one whose marriage you could possibly wreck."

The look on Natasha's face stopped Felicia in her tracks. "I was just kidding. You have never been touchy about the subject, but we haven't spoken in forever . . . stop me I can't figure it out!"

Natasha slowly turned and sat at the edge of the sofa. The same blank stare was plastered on her face by the time Felicia took a seat next to her. Felicia grabbed her hand with right hand and rubbed Natasha's back with her left. It irritates Natasha that Felicia was touchy-feely, but in college, she was like the mother everyone needed away from home. She used the same embrace to make the biggest jocks cry and pour their hearts out. "What's the matter, chick? It can't be that bad. You look like you saw a ghost."

"Just before you got here, Janet and I were on the phone. Everyone all day has been in my ear about my relationships . . . relationship. It has finally driven me crazy."

"What do you mean exactly?"

"Landry was on my case about Bruce. Janet and I were arguing before you came, same topic. When I hung up the phone, I began to feel extremely guilty, and I had a minor panic attack. As I began to calm down, everything was very still and quiet. Then all of a sudden, this whisper comes out of nowhere saying, 'My Word says, "Thou shall not commit adultery."'"

Felicia puckered her lips and nodded slowly, "Sounds like you had a talk with The Maker."

"Who?" Natasha asked with tense brows staring Felicia directly in her eyes.

"God, Father of Jesus, Maker of creation. You know, *God*."

"No, I really don't. My folks didn't bring me up on that stuff, so forgive me of my ignorance."

"I keep a small Bible in my purse of the New Testament. Here you can start with this." Felicia reached in her purse and pulled out her little white Bible that was worn from use. "I will buy you a new one."

"I don't want to know God. I just want to live my life!"

"He is the reason you are yet alive with the stuff you do and the people you have messed over through the years. You should praise King Jesus that you are not burning in hell right now."

"I am not as bad as some."

"Girl, you do not remember half of the things you have done. One, you are sleeping with your boss, who is married. Two, in college you stole some girl's fiancé and slept with him in the back of that girl's car, and you wanted her to see at the rehearsal dinner for crying aloud. Three, there is the occasional black male of wealthy businessman for hush money. Need I say more? I think you are in desperate need of a dose of G-O-D! If everyone is in your face all in one day is just God's way of applying pressure. Words of *wisdom*, it is better to fold than to have God make you obey. When I give you the full Bible, Jonah is the first book I want you to read. What are you going to do about that hair since I see you have tuned me out?"

Natasha sprang to her feet saying, "We have to get going."

Chapter Four

The occasional business celebration would include cheap deli sandwiches and off-brand juice; however, this was not occasional, nor is Peagles your off-brand company. Everything the company does, they do it with class. Every party thrown is the social event in the city. Those given an invitation are allowed one guest, and as always it is a black-tie event. Sponsors and celebrities are among the A-list, and it is up to Peagles to keep the name in the buzz of those who matter and in good light of the press.

Natasha and Felicia arrived fashionably late. Felicia has the body of a model and a face with the inability to take a bad picture. Her fair skin complexion has never seen a blemish, and her hourglass figure is fit for the cover of Vogue magazine. By the looks of her, you can tell she lives in Manhattan. Her living isn't earned off her husband alone. Felicia happens to be the best stockbroker on the floor. No one can do what she does, and everyone at the firm knows it. She gives all the credit to God, who she says, "Keeps her on her A game." Natasha by herself is threatening enough with the singles at the office, but when she and Felicia are together, it is double the troubles. Felicia decided on a simple piece of elegance designed by Bashley Mishka. The one-shoulder-strap green silk gown danced around her curves with every step she took. Felicia made sure she kept her patent leather Fendi clutch in her left hand to draw attention to the six-carrot wedding set that rest on her finger. She wore her hair straight with long layers to give her face definition and her hair volume.

Natasha always stunning and at Felicia's left grabbing with grace a flute glass off the tray of the passing waiter. The bronze goddess always knows how to perfectly match colors to accent her skin tone. The plum strapless dress suited Natasha's shapely figure. The chiffon wings from the empire waist gave the illusion that she walked on air. At least, that is the fantasy Jeffrey had as he caught a glimpse of her entrance. Then she vanished into the crowd of black suits and white linen tables. It was made known earlier that she worked at Peagles. Ashley Brooke, his cousin and Bruce's secretary, had to invite him, given the twenty-one questions he asked about Natasha. For Ashley, he was also a great diversion to get Natasha right where she wanted her. He knew to fall back and watch from a distance until the time was right to approach her. Jeffrey wanted Natasha where it was just she and him that way she would have to talk.

The live band played a variety of music mostly done by request. There were quite a few people on the dance floor getting to know each other a little better with the help of the Cristal. Natasha made a beeline to Bruce's table, introducing herself to the new sponsors and reintroducing her to the old ones. Felicia nodded her head to the right indicating the direction in which she was to go. Natasha nodded back with a confirmation. Mourna Wilson, Bruce's wife, was nowhere in sight making it easy for Natasha getting in and out with introductions without any awkwardness.

Thirty minutes went by before Natasha had enough of the fake laughs and boring jokes. She excused herself and began to walk away, not before seeing Bruce wink at her as he gave her the once-over. This exit was perfect timing for another onlooker who stood patiently a few feet away awaiting the perfect moment to spark up a conversation. Natasha walked two feet before she was practically in the arms of Jeffrey Pattman. He looked even better than she remembered from earlier that afternoon. His hair perfectly lined, and the Versace suit fit him like a glove. If she could cast her vote immediately, he would be on the cover of GQ and have a centerfold just for her. Pretending he didn't mean to run into her, he apologized, "I am so sorry. Are you okay?" There were a few seconds of silence. Natasha had to moisten her mouth with the wine, which had become warm for holding it so long.

"I am fine, but my pedicure isn't. Are you stalking me?"

"No, why would you think that?"

"Well, I see you earlier today at my cousin's restaurant and you just happen to show up at my business party."

"I met Melvin months ago, and his place became one of my regular spots. Tonight my cousin asked me to attend with her. You may know her, Ashley Brooke?"

"Yes, Bruce's secretary."

"It is great that you are talking tonight. Maybe I could get you to dance with me."

The statement caught Natasha off guard. Her palms began to sweat, and she forgot to breathe. Jeffrey reached out his hand and grabbed hers taking her silence as a yes. His touch gave her a sense of comfort. He didn't have beastly man hands like Bruce or any of the others she had encountered. His hands were firm and gentle giving Natasha a security that she has longed for in another, giving her what she has missed in her life. Jeffrey watched Natasha as she conducted herself in that mob of men handling business. He knew the best time to get her was when she couldn't talk her way out of it. He led her to the middle of the floor and turned to look back at her to make sure she didn't display the same look she gave earlier or a look of disapproval. Jeffrey was pleased to find a smirk at the sides of her mouth. They looked one another in the eyes as music began to slow and the melody of the saxophone became apparent. A waiter was passing when Jeffrey got his attention and prepared to take Natasha's drink asking, "May I." She gave him a nod of approval. The waiter scurried off as his mission was accomplished. Jeffrey stepped in closer to Natasha placing his right hand at her waist and his left hand into her right. She didn't know where to put her free hand with Jeffrey being this close. He took his hand from her waist and gently guided her left arm caressingly in the direction that would place it on his right shoulder and then returning his hand back to its place.

"You look stunning."

"Thank you. You look handsome yourself." Natasha couldn't believe her reply. Usually she would give her famous "I know" or say nothing at all. This was neither her usual situation nor the usual guy. This was something she and Felicia were going to talk about all night. Whenever Natasha had a company function, Felicia always went to have her back. Felicia wasn't the only person watching Natasha. Bruce saw the moves Jeffrey put on Natasha. The look of disgust and disappointment couldn't be more obvious unless you were Mrs. Wilson who watched her husband from a few feet away and who finally figured out who had her husband's affection these past few years.

"Can I ask if I could see you again?"

"Sure, but do you expect an answer?"

"I tell you what. We will see how this next song goes. If the conversation is good, we can exchange cards and get to know each other a little better."

"And if it goes sour?"

"We can pretend we never met."

The two had never been in such enjoyment of the presence of another. An hour had passed, and it only seemed like a few minutes to them. They laughed, talked, and decided they would like to continue the conversation. Felicia came up to interrupt. Natasha introduced her friend to Jeffrey. He didn't give her a second look, and Felicia noticed he was all into Natasha. She gave her stamp of approval. The passion burning in their eyes was undeniable, and their experience unforgettable. One can only hope that the events to come will only make their bond stronger.

Chapter Five

It is early. Especially considering how Natasha spends her Sundays. Sleeping until noon, a run in the park, shopping, and a million other things she could think of off the top of her head. Yet here they are, she and Landry driving up to the Billingsworth Estate. Natasha is not in good company due to the fact Landry has been on her Blackberry since the doors automatically locked. This is to be expected since Landry has a fashion show in approximately eight hours. She left her assistant and stylist-in-charge to get the lineup together. Landry was up until four in the morning fitting models and preparing the lineup for the garments. It amused Natasha to hear Landry using the fashion lingo. This gave Natasha some time to think. A reflection on last night with all the commotion made Natasha fearful and joyful. "Was I really hearing the voice of God?" she asked herself. "Why after twenty-eight years tell me how to live and what he says? Just like a deadbeat dad who's trying to get back into their daughter's life." The voice played with the emotions of fear and anger. Fear because Natasha just might have been wrong to think God was not there, and He didn't care about her. Anger because He didn't defend and protect her from the predators that stole her innocence.

She shook her head to throw the thoughts as far from her mind as possible. Landry was startled and checked her face to see if she was okay. The concern vanished when Landry noticed a joyful smirk on Natasha's face. "Let me call you back," said Landry without taking her eyes off Natasha.

Natasha still had the quirky grin on her face not noticing that Landry had completely turned toward her with her back against the door.

"Tell me all about him and leave nothing out."

"What?" Natasha didn't notice she was being watched. Hearing Landry's voice broke her thoughts.

"The reason for that silly grin you have on your face. You don't have that face when you get your bonus. Spill it!"

"All right, DG private eye last night was the company party . . ."

"This I already know, tha good stuff, tha good stuff!"

"Didn't you tell me not to leave anything out?"

"Sorry, continue."

"Thank you, like I was saying. Felicia and I went to the company party as always. I had to entertain the group of big wigs and Bruce. I'm not sure if Mourna, Bruce's wife, was there. This made the night a smooth transaction."

"I know that grin didn't come from Bruce or the fact his wife wasn't around."

"I am getting to that. As I turned to walk away from the boring group of Salt and Peppers, guess who was on my Pedi."

"For heaven's sake, *please* tell me!"

"Jeffrey . . ."

"Who's Jeffrey, the guy from Nerge yesterday afternoon cutie in the tailored suit?"

"That's the one. We danced, talked, and exchanged cards. He isn't like any other guy I have ever encountered."

"Of course not, he chose you not the other way around. Usually, you scope them out, check their accounts, get some dirt, make sure it is solid, and go in for the kill. I don't think I have witness you ever being in a real relationship."

"I haven't . . . that's not the point. I do not trust men, period!"

"What makes him different? We're getting closer to your folks, and I do not have time for anything else but what makes him different?"

"He is charming, has gentle hands, listens, and can reply with something educated that doesn't refer to female anatomy. That is intimidating for me, and it makes me nervous."

"This is new for you. I noticed when he introduced himself at Nerge, and you had nothing sarcastic or self-centered to say he *must* have something going to leave you speechless. It's great to see you bubbly. I know now you have a heart. For a long time, I didn't know."

"Thanks for your honesty."

As the two of them approached the gate, they noticed nothing has changed. Maintenance has been kept, and the estate looks like a photograph out of Home and Gardens. Natasha didn't want to enter the place that brought her such misery. The birth of all her fears and mistrust started right here. She felt like the little girl who had no voice and no choice all over again. As she smiled at Landry, she knew that telling her secret would encourage pity, which is what she needs from no one.

Chapter Six

The door swung open before they could turn the knob. Bryant Billingsworth stood in the open door with open arms and a smile big and bright enough to light the neighborhood in a power outage. Natasha was surprised to see that her father looked as if he hadn't aged a day since she had last seen him five years prior. Dressed in a four-piece suit and never with a hair out of place, he always looked as if he was going to work. The broadness of his shoulders and his height would intimidate anyone, and did. When he came into the room, everyone fell silent, and all heads turned in anticipation making sure they didn't miss a word.

"You made it," exclaimed Bryant embracing the girls at the same time and kissing their foreheads.

"Dad, I can't breathe"

"Oh, sorry honey, I just haven't seen you in what felt like forever."

"Awh, picture perfect. Where is Mrs. B?" asked Landry feeling a little awkward and left out.

"She's in the kitchen, dear."

"You got to move to let us in, Dad. We didn't have breakfast, so we are starving."

A surge of irritation came over Natasha as she entered the Estate. The history that lies in these walls became a staggering weight on her shoulders. Flashes of her childhood set a sickening feeling of disgust in the pit of her stomach. By the time she reached Landry and her mother in the kitchen, she was ready to leave.

Mrs. Michelle Billingsworth and Landry had dishes in hand and headed for the sunroom when Natasha entered the kitchen.

"My god, you are more beautiful than I remembered. Come here, child," sang Michelle. She sat the dishes on the island in passing and floated across the room with her arms wide open anticipating Natasha's embrace. Natasha gave a one-arm hug with the look of revulsion on her face. Michelle knew this same reaction from Natasha all too well, "Come, help with the rest of the dishes," softly demanded Michelle.

The sunroom has the same furnishings since the Billingsworth took residence. Everything is like new since the room sees little visitors. Bryant is the only one with friends and a social circle. Michelle managed to keep to herself throughout their marriage. The small talk and number exchange made between wives at the company parties go short-lived. Michelle would not allow herself to cackle among women because of her insecurities. No one was going to take her wealth from under her nose. Foolish women needed a troop. All Michelle needed was herself.

When the women were done setting the table Michelle insisted that they have a seat and that Bryant join them. Landry looked at Natasha with confusion and mouthed, "What's she doing?" Natasha sat down and shrugged while she looked on. Bryant made himself comfortable with his back to the sun at the six-seat round table. Natasha sat to Bryant's right with a seat between them and Landry to her right. It startled Landry to see Mrs. Billingsworth placing food on the table but not as much as it did Natasha. Bryant chuckled at the look on their faces and commented, "You look like it's a stranger serving you the plague. Your mother got rid of Rosaline and has put on her domestic cap, which I haven't seen in decades, odd to me too girls."

Three trips are what it took Michelle before the family had a traditional southern spread before them. There were mashed potatoes, English peas, cornbread, candy yams, collard greens, fried chicken, turkey, and pumpkin pie for dessert. Natasha couldn't remember her mother in the kitchen doing anything but making a pot of coffee and making reservations. Finally, on the last round, Michelle had a seat to Bryant's left letting out a sigh of relief. Everyone peered into Michelle's face mostly because they had never seen her break a sweat, and here she was with the appearance of a housewife who had cooked a large meal for her loved ones. A look of surprise on Michelle's face was what the family received back with the demand, "Landry bless the food, and ya'll stop looking at me like ya crazy." Landry gave an eye roll and blurted," Why must I always bless the food?" Michelle looked at her with piercing eyes surprised that she would even think of questioning her. Landry caught her gaze and immediately started with grace, "Dear Lord, bless this food we are about to receive. Let it fill our bellies as well as our hearts in this time of fellowship with our loved ones. Lord, bless those who are less fortunate than us. Be with those who cannot feed themselves. Supply all of their need. Amen"

Natasha looked upon the faces of those at the table with racing thoughts while Landry prayed. It is automatic when someone is praying to bow your head, but Natasha could not follow the custom. There was so much hatred toward her mother that it is taking everything in her to be in her presence. She doesn't know how she made it through her adolescence in the same house as Michelle. Michelle was less than a mother and nowhere near a saint. "It is just brunch . . . one-hour brunch," Natasha whispered to herself.

Bryant heard the muffle and asked, "Did you say something, dear?"

"Just repeating to myself the things I have to do when I get to the office."

"You can forget the office for a second and spend time with us. We haven't seen you in ages, and even that was for a second. I have an idea why don't we plan a family vacation, Landry, you too. We can go to the mountains or to the beach. It will also give you two a chance to bring gentlemen because I know neither of you lovely ladies are single in that city."

Landry giggled and said through blushing eyes, "I am not seeing anyone, and I like the way you put it to make it seem as if you weren't being nosy. After tonight, I don't know when I will see an off-day, beach, or gentlemen. Natasha is due for some R and R after her campaign."

Upset at the fact, Landry put the spotlight on her. Natasha clenched her teeth to the point of pain.

"Well, Nat, what do you say," inquired Michelle.

Natasha exhaled to reduce the frustration she was feeling before she answered the question with a firm, "No."

"I tell you, child, your acting like being with your family is the worst thing in the world. I am sure that we did not raise you to be so antisocial with us or anyone else. What is your problem?"

Natasha leaned forward in her chair and peered directly into her mother's eyes. She prepared her mouth to let everything she was feeling burst out like a broken levy, but the words were interrupted by her father's statement.

"I am dying. I would like it if you did not tear into our daughter on her decisions and for the both of you to be able to converse as people who have the same blood pumping through their veins before I leave this earth."

"Dad, what's wrong?"

"Cancer is what is wrong. I do not have long but with the time I do have I would like to spend it enjoying the days I have been left with those close to me. I have set in place those who will be responsible for my business and have made sure all is in order, so none of you will have to worry. Natasha, you will have a place there if you so desire, but I know you have your own life and name. I was hoping this would be a happy gathering, and I could put the news to you all at another time, but since the atmosphere was going sour, I might as well add the salt."

Chapter Seven

The news at brunch threatened to shatter the evening's events. The beat of the city put Natasha at ease in Landry's loft apartment. She watched people racing with somewhere to go and no time to get there. Fashion Ave within one block brings out the most creative wardrobes and the best and worst dress list. Natasha's thoughts set in on what her father said, and he was right. She and her mother have a relationship that is clearly dysfunctional. They cannot be in the room together without nearly plucking each other's eyes out. The scenery outside the loft windows faded into the distance, and all Natasha could see was darkness. The darkness became so concentrated that everything became as black as the bottom of a well, and she was trapped in the bottom. It became hard for Natasha to breathe. She fell to her knees grabbing her throat and desperately gasping for air. In the mist of the suffocating experience, Natasha heard the whimpering of a child, then suddenly the voice of a man saying, "Her mother may be done, but we have a clean rug to wipe our feet on boys. Your mother doesn't care about you. All she cares about is your father's money."

Natasha's eyes began to swell with the ocean of tears threatening to spew over the lids. She recognized that voice in the darkness. That voice makes her feel seven years old all over again. The voice took her innocence and caused the rift in the relationship with her mother. That same voice that made her beg Bryant Billingsworth not to leave her with her mother and to take her with him whenever he left the house. That voice belonged to one of Michelle's many lovers but the one of four who took turns defiling her innocent body. When reaching the realization that this was an occurrence that happened more than once and one that she never dealt with, Natasha didn't know how to handle it. She curled into the fetal position in the floor and wept helpless taking what breaths she could between sobs. Before she knew it, there were people standing around her with only one familiar face, Landry's. Her mouth was moving, but Natasha heard no words just still silence of a calm atmosphere in all the chaos. Then a still small voice called to her, "Natasha." Seconds later, a command, "Just breathe." Natasha's body reacted in an instance, her lungs filling with air, and the color returned to her face. Landry's voice became clear as a bell. She was praying, "Dear God, help her in the name of Jesus whatever it is. Fix it, Master, fix it."

*   *   *

Wrapped in a blanket and balled on the sofa, Natasha sat watching the people watch her as if she were a lunatic. Landry made haste in her direction with a cup of hot tea in her hand. After handing the smoking cup to Natasha, Landry sat next to her moving the stray strands from her face. She waited a few moments before asking the obvious.

"What happened, sweetie? One minute, you were laughing at the street walkers' ensembles. The next minute, you are on the floor like a fish out of water. Talk to me."

"I feel better, really I do. We have four hours until showtime, and I will escort you like I said I would."

"Natasha let's be serious . . . that was a panic attack like I have never seen. You mean to tell me you are going to treat it like it's nothing."

"I am not saying it's nothing. I am just saying it is not something I want to deal with right now."

"That is the problem, Nat, you're not dealing. It only gets worse from here. You need to face your problems head-on, and let Jesus help you. He helped me with all my problems, and one day, you and I will really talk. I'm not going to force you share in this particular situation. I will give you until tomorrow, and then you spill, agreed?"

"Agreed. They almost have everything out of here, huh?"

"Yes. This is a one-hundred-and-fifty garment fashion show. The dressers and steamers, better be ready, because they are going to work tonight."

"I am so proud of you, Dry Greens."

"Thanks for being there for me. There will not be a dry seat in the house. I have investors and buyers coming from overseas as well as store owners from Tokyo, Paris, Milan, Barcelona, and other places that I need to remember when it is time for the meet and greet. Are you sure you are up to being my right-hand girl?"

"I am sure. I will put my A game forward, and I will not disappoint you, or have any other emotional outburst."

Chapter Eight

Total chaos is the only thing that explains the backstage area of the fashion show. The music is blasting; Landry is meeting with the dressers and lineup crew to make sure everything is on point and ready to roll. There are twenty-five models pacing to find their picture on the racks of clothes so that they can see where they would be and what they are wearing. Natasha has never been present at the birthing of a clothing line. She has only witnessed the creations of designers like Christian Lacrox, Bill Blass, Elie Tahari, and Oscar de la Renta in the front row in arm's reach of "A" list celebrities. Natasha went up the short stairway to the runway imagining herself draped in her favorite of Landry's collection, a plum silk gown that has cap sleeves and drapes her curves like a dream; the chiffon wings that hang from the empire waist leaves a ten-foot train that dances through the air when it catches the wind.

Her imagination was interrupted by the sound of someone clearing their throat. She opened her eyes to find guests had started to arrive and the chairs were almost full. The height of her embarrassment came when she discovered who broke her daydream. Jeffrey stood to the right of the runway with a schoolboy grin on his face that made Natasha blush in embarrassment. "And scene," Jeffrey said, as he chuckled. He gave Natasha the once-over starting at her feet then back up to her face. She couldn't help but notice that his eyes on her gave this tingling sensation on her skin as if his eyes were his hands gently caressing her body. Natasha's body heat began to rise as their eyes met just as they did when she first saw him in Nerge and the night they danced. It pleased her to find that turn at the corner of his mouth giving his approval of her appearance. "Stunning" was the word Jeffrey used to compliment Natasha as he reached out his hand to help her down the side stairs. Natasha dropped her head in a coy manner reaching for his hand but before their fingers could entangle into one, Landry came from the backstage out of breath.

"Girl, Mayday! Six of the models didn't show, and I only booked five stand-ins. I need one more hanger."

"What are you going to do, and why a hanger?" Natasha asked with a look of panic and confusion.

"That would be you. You tried on the dress, and you looked great in it. You are fierce enough to bring it to life for the closing of the show."

"What?"

"All you have to do is be your confident self, walk down the runway, pose at the end, and then come back. When it is all done, all the models will walk out together. Then you and I will walk out together, piece of cake!"

"I have seen a ton of fashion shows, some girls fall, and some girls need not do it again. I do not want to be the 'don't-do-it-again girl,' Dry Greens."

"At this point, I have no one else. Please do this for me," Landry asked on her knees with only twenty minutes before show time.

"You won't be mad if I tank?"

"I know you won't embarrass me. I have never seen you in an embarrassing situation where you have fallen or even had anything in your nose or on your face. God, women help me!"

There was such panic in the moment that Natasha forgot Jeffrey was there, and Landry didn't even notice him until he gave a little nudge of encouragement, "You will be perfect, and don't worry about it."

Natasha looked back at Jeffrey with surprise as he peered back at her from the bottom of the side stairs; she gave a smile and agreed to be in the show. Landry jumped to her feet and kissed Natasha's cheek. She took Natasha by the hand and spoke into her headset, "We have our model!"

Natasha's adrenalin was pumping as the models raced past her to change in and out of their clothes. Some of the other models had five different looks which only gave them a few seconds to change. Natasha was glad she was last because she got to see the actual excitement that went on backstage. The dressers were basically pulling the models' clothes on and off making sure everything was according to the photos, then pushing them toward the runway to make sure they fell into their designated position with lineup. It seemed like only seconds had passed, and it was Natasha's time to walk. The makeup artist made sure her face was perfect with the dramatic eye makeup they had decided and was also pleased that it only took five minutes due to her flawless features. Her dresser fluffed her dress and made sure her shoes were strapped.

As Natasha walked toward the runway, she could hear her heart in her ears, and her mind went completely blank. Then suddenly everything became quiet in her mind, and the small voice came and said, "You're the show." When she got to the top of the stairs, Landry was there. "After her, you're next. Don't worry. You are the show. Just walk to the music," Landry said hoping this would boost her confidence. A gun going off in a race is what it felt like when Landry said, "Walk." Automatically, Natasha's feet began to move, and the wind caught her dress. Just as she pictured herself in her daydream was what was manifested on the runway. The gown was a captivating piece in itself, but to put Natasha in it *made* the gown. When she got to the end of the runway, she gave the cameraman a little smirk and turned back leaving all in awe. Her charisma and personality shone through making the show's end an unforgettable one. After the final walk, Landry brought Natasha out with her as she bowed, waved, and blew a kiss to the crowd.

The mixer after the show had its excitement as well. Landry landed the overseas accounts with the buyers, and she established contact with a few European boutique owners that wanted to house *Dry Greens* as one of their brands. She was also extended an invitation to Milan the following month to meet with other industry professionals to take her line there for viewing. Little did Natasha know there was something planned for her all along. As she stood with Jeffrey chatting about the show, Landry walked up with five gentlemen and two women. Natasha excused herself and cleared her throat to introduce herself. A familiar face came into focus in the crowd of suits. Oscar de la Renta walked up to Natasha, kissed her hand, and said to her, "Beautiful, you will hear from me soon." He turned and walked away and the small mob proceeded after him. With their backs turned, Landry turned around behind them giving Natasha thumbs-up and mouthing "Fierce."

Natasha turned toward Jeffrey, with her mouth open in amazement. The climax of excitement brought the two into an embrace so close that they became one. He was intoxicated with the soft mango scent of her hair. His arms found a resting place around her body that brought a sense of security that she longed for since they danced. Jeffrey let out a deep sigh as he held her with her head against his chest. He managed to get up enough nerve to mutter, "It is a must that I take you on a date before Oscar sweeps you off your feet."

For a moment, Natasha forgot to breathe. She knew that sooner or later, she would have to tell him about who she really was and what she did, but for now, she would be free. Natasha looked Jeffrey in the eyes and said, "Name the day and time."

"Wednesday, my church has Bible study from six until seven and after that, we can do what you want. How does that sound?"

"Sounds like a date."

Chapter Nine

Just another day at the office, thought Natasha as she finished her meeting with the marketing team to plan the next big event for Peagles and to strategize the launch of their campaign in China. It is a dreary Monday morning with time passing at a low crawl. Ashley Brooke was parched at her desk awaiting the dismissal of the marketing meeting. Natasha made a specific request that there were to be no disturbances whatsoever during meetings. Ashley stood as soon as she and Natasha made eye contact with a list of calls she missed, one being from her cousin Jeffrey.

"I know it is none of my business, but what's going on with you, two?"

Natasha gave a smug look of surprise which soon turned into irritation. "You're right. It is none of your business."

As Natasha grabbed her messages, Ashley did not loose her grip. The rage in Ashley almost erupted, but she gave her informative statement through clinched teeth, "Mr. and Mrs. Wilson are waiting to meet with you in his office, and enjoy the rest of your day."

The vindictive smile on Ashley's face was undeniable. It was so noticeable that Natasha's stomach turned before she could finish the sentence. Her nerves stood on edge as she approached to cracked door of Bruce Wilson's office. The voices coming from behind the door sounded very unpleasant. Mourna Wilson's razor-sharp words cut like a knife. Talks of divorce and taking him for everything he has are the words that proceeded out of her mouth. Natasha didn't know if she needed to knock or run. She knew that this day would come. *Here goes nothing,* she thought as she knocked on the door.

"Come in," echoed the voice of Bruce with a hint of anger.

As Natasha entered the room, Mrs. Wilson stood with the look of disgust on her face. "Do have a seat," said Mourna directing Natasha to the seat next to her with the manila folder in it. Natasha held her head high preparing her mind for what was about to take place. She grabbed the folder from the seat and waited for Mourna to sit as well. Bruce took a seat behind his desk. Mourna looked at Natasha and said, "You can sit as well. I have something to say." Natasha sat as Mourna instructed and looked Bruce directly in the eyes as to say, "What?"

"No need for the faces until I am done. Something was brought to my attention. Who would have guessed that checking my mail and finding a package that weighed the amount of a newborn could crumble my existence?" Mourna proceeded with her speech pacing back and forth, with her hands clasped together as if she were a college professor. "The strange thing about the package—there was no return address. The content of the package is there in the envelope. Open it."

Natasha took a deep breath and opened the folder. There were pictures. The photos continued for what seemed like a lifetime, hundreds of pictures including Natasha and Bruce in compromising positions. Natasha could tell by the clothes that she wore or didn't wear when the pictures were taken. Some of the photos were taken years prior to the date which gave Natasha an idea of who sent the pictures. *The vindictive smile that set this meeting in motion is the culprit*, she thought. By the time she got to the twentieth photo, she got tired and tossed the folder on Bruce's desk. Natasha clothed herself in her "who cares attitude" and asked, "What do you want from me?"

"Are you kidding me, you slut? What do I want from you? What could you possibly want from another woman's husband? Do you even care about the fact that we have a family or that he and I have been married longer than you have been alive? We have children your age!"

"Mrs. Wilson, to me this is a business arrangement. I am paid for my services which include hours at the office and any overtime that I put in. I was only thinking of myself, and it still stands that self is my number one priority."

"I want her fired! I want her fired right now Bruce!!!"

"Mourna, she is the best at what she does. Since I hired her, sales have been on the incline, and we have had more exposure than this company has ever seen. I am afraid if I get rid of her, the company will do just the opposite of its current trend."

"Well, if you don't fire her, I will tell the press about the bonuses, offshore accounts with money that can't be accounted for, bribes, and any other dirt the investigator dug up."

Bruce looked over at Natasha with a look of surprise. The information Mourna had was the same information Bruce shared with Natasha in their private meetings. Natasha knew that this was the end of her career with Peagles, so before Bruce could open his mouth, Natasha stood and said, "This is my official resignation. Please have my package ready by tomorrow morning, and I will have the resignation in writing."

The doors closing behind Natasha echoed in her mind. Yes, she might have ruined a marriage, but the sense of freedom she gained when she quite went deeper than just leaving her job. She made up her mind that she was leaving the lifestyle altogether. She wanted love, not just the word passed about in the heat of passion that is felt by only one but a love between mutual companions. The things in the past that haunt her from her childhood no longer have her restricted and unable to show emotion. Natasha walked past Ashley with the biggest smile on her face and said, "I am free! Could you please get a few boxes for me so that I can clean out my office?"

Natasha didn't notice the daggers in Ashley's eyes as she went into her office and began to gather her things. Another plan to bring her to her knees was already in effect. Pure hatred was what drove the motives of Ashley Brooke. Her inability to let go and forgive was the perfect brewing to bring turmoil into the life of Natasha. "You may be able to disregard the feelings of one woman scorned, but there will be no escape from her wrath," said Ashley through clinched teeth.

Chapter Ten

A plastic carton of memories is all Natasha carried into her apartment. She left behind anything that would remind her of her life at Peagles. The rewards, photos with celebrities, and plaques were left as is in the office that she left wide open. Natasha felt liberated with the weight of being the mistress lifted off her shoulders. As she sat the carton on the end table and pulled open the curtains to her living room, she turned around to see she had had the same furniture since her first paycheck at Peagles. The rugs, sofas, all of it screamed "trash it" to Natasha's eyes. She looked at her watch to see it was only eleven ten in the morning. With shopping on her mind, she proceeded to her bedroom to shower and change into something more comfortable. Natasha didn't realize her answering machine flashing with messages before she exited her condo on the mission for furnishing. Her phone rang when she proceeded to street level with the message, "Nat, baby your father is ill. It would be great if you turn your cell phone on. Call us on the mobile phone when you get this message."

The first furniture store Natasha came to was the one she stopped in. She went completely against her style of contemporary sheek and bought a lime green sectional, with bronze end and coffee tables, and all the accessories to accent her decision; a seventy-two-inch plasma television will take up the adjacent wall to the sectional. Natasha had never owned a television and it figured today marking a new day. Her bedroom followed the lines of contemporary with a new king-size bed with a leather headboard and bedside tables to accent. Natasha thought *she should keep the antique dressers her father had given her from his mother.* She found a two-seated dining table to replace the existing one. When she went over the paperwork and counted the cost, she was happy with her decision especially when they told her discarding the existing furniture will be of no charge.

Thirty-one thousand dollars is the cost of her condo's facelift. By the time the furniture was assembled in its place and the movers had gone, it was 4:49 p.m. Natasha flopped on her new sofa and let out a breath of achievement. She felt the need to give Landry, Felicia, and Janet a call for an update on her job status. As soon as the thought crossed her mind, her buzzer became an interruption of her delight. Natasha pressed the button to speak, "Who is it?" The responsive voice brought her such joy and one person that she could skip on her phone list. "Open the door, chica!"

Moments later, Janet burst in the door yelling, "Hola America!" They embraced like two friends who had been apart for years. The door was wide open, and the doorman stood after placing Janet's bags by the entrance and awaited his tip. "Oh, sorry, sir. Thank you so much for putting up with my chatting for thirteen floors. Keep the change." Giving the doorman a fifty-dollar bill and a big smile might have made his day. Janet closed the door to turn around and see the changes that had taken place.

"What have you done with the place? There is more color and life. Is this stuff new? It smells like it," said Janet, while stroking the leather and looking around.

"Yes, it is and for other news, I got fired today. No, no correction. I quit!"

"Chica, are you crazy? Why would you do something like that? Okay, you quit as if you walked out, not as if you got escorted out."

"I quit."

Natasha flopped on the new green sofa, with her feet tucked under her. Janet joined her sitting to her right with her elbows on her knees and her chin in her hands. "Spill it," commanded Janet.

"After our morning meeting this morning, I was summoned to Bruce's office."

"What's the matter? He wanted a kinkier afternoon quickie?"

"Let me finish. As soon as I stepped inside, Mourna asked me to have a seat and to look at the photos in a folder that was in the chair."

"Whaaaaaat?"

"Yes. Bruce was just sitting there with a stern face. She went through this whole spill about did I think about their family or her feelings and all this crap I could give a flip about. Then when there was no budging on our part, she went to say she would spill the beans about his extracurricular activities with accounts and bribes and all that blah if he didn't fire me. He tried to keep me, so I just let myself out. I felt so liberated and free when I packed my things and left. No more sex for money under the table and the other perks I got. No more crap from other associates and deadlines, just *stuff*!"

Janet let out a long sigh and said, "That's great. You're free from the company and the baggage you created. It is still shocking to me that you have no conscience about the things you have done. I have to be honest. The things that you have done will put anyone in a confessional for years."

"Emotions are for the weak, and I will not let myself be one of those people."

"I love you, Nat. If you don't let go of what happened to you in the past, whatever it is, you will not have any relationship worth calling a relationship."

"I think you're wrong. Jeffrey Pattman has taken an interest in me, and I in him. We will see what happens. We have a date on Wednesday."

"Who's this mystery man? Don't think you are off the hook with the conversation. Now, can I shower and can you feed me? If you bought furniture, I think, you could foot the bill."

The ladies lugged the bags to the spare bedroom. Janet prepared to take a shower and sang loudly in Spanish. Natasha laughed at her melody which sounded like a prayer for her salvation. She noticed the flashing lights on her answering service and pressed *play*.

Chapter Eleven

Natasha's legs couldn't move fast enough as she ran down the echoing hallways of the hospital. Janet was clacking behind in mix-matched stilettos and wet hair. Michelle was sitting at the end of the hallway with a coffee in her hand and a strong focus on the pale wall in front of her. The commotion startled her and brought her to her feet. She walked at a fast pace to meet them. Natasha had never seen her mother so undone. Michelle's appearance was of a woman who had nothing or who had just lost everything.

"Where's Daddy?" asked Natasha as she fought back her tears.

All Michelle could do to answer was point to the room with the open door and the sound of machinery. Mrs. Billingsworth took her place in the chair adjacent to the door as if she never moved when Natasha and Janet entered the room hand in hand. Never had Natasha seen her father ill. She couldn't recall him ever having the flu or other common illnesses. Strong and reliant was Bryant Billinsworth. Her breath left her when she saw the tubings and monitors. She fell into Janet's bosom and wept. As she sobbed, there came stillness over her, a comforting silence that blanketed her with ease. Then a still small voice came and said, "Yes, his health will fade, and he will join Me, but I am not taking him now. Things must be brought out, and you must spend time with your father. He is the only one you will have aside Me."

Four nurses had come and gone as Natasha and Janet sat in the room waiting. The air was thick with silence, with the occasional grunt of Michelle in the hallway clearing her throat. A few moments went by in the silence until it was interrupted by a gurgling rumble. Janet grabbed her stomach to silence it, but it was too late. Natasha looked at her in disbelief and giggled saying, "We were on our way to dinner before the news. I'm not hungry. Will you ask my mother if she wants anything? Here's my wallet." Janet received the wallet and gripped Natasha's hand saying, "I will bring you back a coffee anyway since you're paying. Be strong lovely. I will return shortly and less noisy." Natasha returned the squeeze and said, "Thank you."

Janet left the room making a pit stop at Michelle to make sure she was okay and if she wanted anything. Surprising enough for Janet, Michelle agreed to go with her. Except for Landry, Michelle rarely met any of Natasha's friends. Michelle thought chatting with Janet might take her mind away from the event, even if it is just for a little while.

As the sound of Janet's stilettos began to be at the pitch of a whisper, Natasha drew her chair in closer to Bryant studying his face. The rise and fall of his chest as he breathed let her know that he was still with her. She put her face close to his ear and began to say, "Dad, I love you. I should have visited more, told you I love you more, and just been around more. I let the past affect our relationship, and you had nothing to do with the chaos. Things were quieter when you were around and more like a home, but when you left for business, it took a totally different turn. The mask came off those who you're supposed to trust to protect, and they lived different lives. Lies, all lies, Daddy. I wish you could see through them. I wish I could tell you the things that happened . . ."

Natasha's conversation was interrupted by Bryant's explosive sneeze. Natasha panicked and pressed the nurse's button. Dr. Richard was in the room by the seventh sneeze and to see Bryant's eyes wide open. Dr. Richard removed the breathing tub from his nostrils and began asking a series of questions, "What is your name?" Bryant looked the doctor in the eyes and answered, "Bryant Billingsworth, and what's your name?" Dr. Richard chuckled and answered, "I am Dr. Richard. Do you know where you are?" Bryant laughed and said, "I guess in the hospital if you're a doctor and I'm on the stretcher. My daughter standing in the corner looking at me like I am the dead rising. Don't worry sweetie. I am on a brain-free diet." The room erupted into laughter for a moment, but Dr. Richard brought things back to focus with his last question, "Do you know what happened to you?" Bryant looked at Dr. Richard with the same assurance he had when he told him his name and said, "Well, Dr. Richard, I have cancer. I have lost forty pounds, and no one noticed. If I were a woman, this would be a good thing. I know I am dying, and I believe the reason for my short stay here is that my wife accidentally gave me Viagra. Now, can I go on vacation before my last day arrives?" Dr. Richard looked at him with a half smile and answered, "You are going to have to stay a day or two so that we can make sure you're well enough to leave." Bryant huffed as if he were a disappointed child, folded his arms and said, "Doc, you're telling me I have to stay here to see if I am well enough to leave when you know I am going to die sooner than later. Please correct me if I am wrong or did you just not think before those words came out of your mouth? Better yet, call Dr. Mitchell Montgomery, my primary physician. He is in Aruba, where I was hoping to get to before I die."

Natasha couldn't help being tickled by the fact her father never lost his touch of being able to make people do what he wanted. She remembered him taking conference calls, those brief moments at home, and the same forceful tone he used that made people do exactly what he asked. His ability to make the most professional men feel inadequate in their expertise was a gift Natasha herself had attained from this brilliant businessman.

Dr. Richard excused himself to make the phone call, and the two nurses that entered before him followed after. Natasha came to her father's bed and grabbed his hand.

"Why did you have to be so rude with the doctor?"

"I am here for a limited time only, and there are a few things we must address as a family before I go. Telling you I have cancer was shock enough. I do not want everything else to be likewise."

"What else could there possibly be?"

"Well, I have other children in the Hamptons, two boys to be exact."

Chapter Twelve

The normal family would think the weather is perfect for vacation. The transition from Summer to Autumn makes for great picnics and barbeques. Waterfront properties are hard to come by this time of year, but as always Bryant called a friend, and an hour later, the Billingsworths were in their private jet, headed to their destination. Natasha was appalled by the information her father laid in her lap the previous day. By the looks of Michelle, she received the same news. Natasha couldn't help but think that the information was the cause in the mix-up of medication. A million other thoughts ran through Natasha's mind, like what else she didn't know about. Her father, out of the little family she had, would be the least likely to keep secrets. When Natasha thought about it even more, she came to the realization that her father wasn't at home enough to make any big errors in her life. He could've easily lied about anything, and no one would ever know the difference. Her mind was running like a hamster on a wheel to the point where she didn't know they had landed and preparing to exit the plan. The sounds of her fathers' voice interrupted her thinking. "If you do not come now, they lock you in with no food or water, but you have all the wine you want," joked Bryant.

Upon their arrival to the beach house, Michelle was obviously disappointed. Anything less than twelve bedrooms was beneath her. Her taste in her present life hid the fact that Michelle was brought up on dirt roads and an outhouse in poor dung Mississippi. She snarled and said, "You mean to tell me we couldn't get anything bigger?"

Bryant sat in front with the driver to converse about manly things such as sports. When he heard Michelle's question, the hairs on his neck stood on end, and he said through his teeth, "Never grateful and never satisfied." The car was silent enough to hear laughing from a neighboring house.

The S-class Mercedes in the driveway caught everyone's attention, but it only seems to matter to Natasha and Michelle. Bryant carried one bag, and the driver carried the rest to the house. The women followed a few feet behind and were appalled to see that Bryant got out his personal keys and used one to unlock the door. Bryant looked back at the women and said, "Don't look too surprised. The people living here are my people and yours too, for that matter." Two men who appeared to be around Natasha's age came to the door and grabbed two bags for Bryant and the driver. They introduced themselves as Bryant Jr., who is the elder one, and Nathanel, the younger one. Natasha figured that she was due to wake up at any moment.

The homelike feeling when Natasha entered the house was something she had always longed for. Plenty of family photos were hanging as they walked through the foyer. There was no mistaking who lived in this house. Bryant Jr. looked like Mr. Billingsworth in his younger years. Michelle couldn't hold back the tears that streamed down her face. They seemed so happy and were smiling in every picture. There were even pictures of Mr. Billingsworth. Michelle could tell his age by the length of his hair and the style of suit in each photograph. As they approached the kitchen, the sound of water running and dishes clanking were apparent. Michelle grabbed her chest and had all hope that the only other person to meet was the maid, but to her disappointment stood just the opposite. Bryant reached the kitchen first and was standing with the other woman. "Meet Tessa Townsen, mother of Bryant Jr. and Nathanel," said Bryant with a big smile on his face.

"This is really happening?" is all Natasha could say in her mind. The dinner table was set and Tessa asked if they would sit down. They would be staying four days in the house of her father's mistress with two men who were her brothers. The dinner table was full of delectables, but only the people who resided there and had been there before were eating. Michelle had the same blank stare that she had in the hospital, and Natasha had her elbow propped on the table, with her head resting on her fists observing the family that sat in front of her. They were chatting so intensely that they forgot the visitors at the table. Bryant asked, "Natasha, Michelle, are you going to eat anything?"

Natasha fired at Bryant, "At this moment, I can't believe my eyes. I am sitting here in a place with people I have never been with and I hadn't a clue existed until yesterday, and you expect me to do what? I feel like I'm in a soap opera."

Bryant replied with concern in his voice, "I know this is too much to take at any moment, and my only regret is not telling you sooner. It is actually unfair because Tessa knew of you and your mother, and she let the boys know about you too. I didn't let her reach out to you because of how you and your mother were getting along. I have never looked for a father or husband of the year award, and I can't say that I have regret in my actions because two children became of it. I was just too much of a coward to tell you both, and for that I am sorry."

The mounts of disgust threatened to spill out of Natasha's mouth; however, not toward her father and his actions but her actions days prior and the years leading to this point. She ran to the restroom and unleashed years of pain she had caused to other families. Like Tessa, she was fully aware of what she was doing, and didn't care about who may get hurt. Mourna was one of the many faces that came to Natasha's mind as she heaved every memory. Thirteen faces of men who were in relationships that Natasha damaged or broke proceeded thereafter. "God, forgive me," pleaded Natasha.

Later that night, Natasha went into the guest room, where her mother was lying on the bed. The first time in her life Natasha felt compassion and remorse for someone else who she was hurting. She wasn't the friend to call on when there was relationship trouble, but for everything else she had you covered. Tonight, she would let go of the hatred she had for her mother and do her best to comfort her. Natasha climbed in bed behind Michelle and held her weeping mother. Michelle began to mutter her secrets and regrets saying, "I haven't been much of a wife. I haven't been faithful as well." Natasha gave an eye roll she couldn't resist. "Not in all my years would I have thought he'd have another family—an entire life that we had no clue about. Nat, I married your father for his money, but I fell in love with him eventually," continued Michelle, "I robbed myself of real love and happiness, and I forbid you do the same."

Natasha was not prepared for the advice her mother gave her. Only one person came into mind. Jeffrey Pattman, the man that made time stop whenever they were together, the man whose smile she could lose herself in, the man whose embrace brought security, and the one man she ever considered to be her husband. Natasha's heart marked him the man she would never share. Wednesday is only ten hours away, and even though her father is ill, it pained her that she wouldn't see him.

After two hours of sobbing, Michelle was finally asleep. Natasha crept out of bed to locate her iPhone and tell Janet of the happenings. She found herself feeling awkward in the house of strangers, but nevertheless made her way to the sunroom to have a private conversation. As she walked the dim hallway, she heard the television in the family room blaring and chuckles from her father and the boys. The light from her phone shined upon her face as she scrolled through the phonebook. Passing a mirror, she saw her mascara had run. She had to pass the family room to get to the patio, and she didn't want anyone to know she had cried with her mother. Natasha also noticed the icky taste in her mouth. The decision to take care of her hygiene became first priority.

Natasha made it to the sunroom in one piece. She thought if she didn't make eye contact with anyone she would be home free. When she shut the door behind her, she turned to find Tessa sitting in the corner reading. "Well, my dear, you have just stumbled upon my favorite place of the house," said Tessa in a matter-of-fact tone. "I just wanted to make some calls and think," replied Natasha. Natasha thought to herself, "Why the hell am I giving an explanation to this gold digging whore who doesn't deserve one." The thought was true but cut like a knife because Natasha was sure so many women had wanted to say similar things to her. "Okay, but I just want to say as bad as this is I paid for this house, the car in the driveway, and all of my possessions. I fell in love with your father two years after he and your mother wedded. You were only two. It is and was wrong, but I couldn't let him divorce your mother. She was the spotlight housewife, and I was the independent rebel. The only thing your father purchased was an education for the boys. Bryant Jr. is twenty-five years old, which makes him three years younger than you, and Nathanel is twenty-three. I didn't hide the truth from them because I hate secrets, *but* your father made me keep this one from you all these years. They know your accomplishments and what you do from your father. Hopefully, if you find it in your heart to forgive us, things will be better. I am truly sorry for what was done, but I can't completely be sorry because my sons came from it." Tessa rose to her feet. The light from the house made her fair-complexioned skin radiant. Her almond-shaped eyes had sorrow in them, but her lips parted a smile. Tessa stood at five foot seven inches of exactly what Natasha didn't want to become. Yes, her father was away quite a bit in her life, but knowing you will always be second string will never make amends.

The door closed behind Natasha, and she peered around the room for a moment taking in what was said. The room was decorative with five-piece wicker furniture set. Two ferns hang from the ceiling above each armrest of the loveseat facing the door. A wide-bottom wicker chair and matching ottoman is to the left of the door and look-alike to the right side of the door. Five giant windows reveal the beach that is only fifteen hundred yards away. The lime green cushions tickle Natasha because it made her think of her new furniture at home that she hasn't had the chance to break in. Natasha decided to take this time to break out of her rules, and before she knew it, her fingers hit *Send*. The receiver echoed three rings before a familiar female voice interrupted her nervousness.

"Hello," said Ashley Brooke.

"May I speak to Jeffrey, and hi Ashley," replied Natasha thinking next time she would only call his cell phone.

"Hold, whore. Now I am going to take this time to let you know who I really am. This has been coming years in the making, but since you quit Peagles, my job is no longer at steak for speaking my mind. A more familiar name to you just might be Christopher Hurston," snarled Ashley. "There is no reply, so you must have forgotten the name of the man who you slept with in the backseat of his fiancé's car. Let me tell you what it cost me—miscarriage from stress, twenty additional pounds, and therapy. I know money comforts you, but nothing comforts my pain. I feel much better now that you know what you have done and who I am. Now ask yourself, 'How do I sleep at night?' Oh, here is Jeffrey."

Natasha found it hard to breathe. She could see Ashley's face with the additional baby pounds and the look of heart break. Her thoughts were going a mile a minute when she heard Jeffrey questioning, "Is it true? You are the girl that made my cousin lose her baby?" Natasha removed her hand from her chest as she said in reply, "I am the guilty party with no explanation, just sorry." There was a moment of complete silence. Natasha's heart raced with anticipation of what he would say and just how damaged this whole thing could be. Before she knew it, she commanded, "Let me talk to Ashley, if she will let me?" The atmosphere of the conversation brought such tension that Natasha had to sit down. Moments went by before Ashley spoke into the receiver saying through tears, "I always rehearsed what I would say when I saw you again and I have hated you for so long. When I got the job at Peagles and the HR manager brought me up to where I would work, your face was the first one to welcome me aboard. My heart dropped to my toes, and all I wanted to do was grab anything I could and take your life. Years have gone by, and today, I finally get the opportunity to tell you what I feel, but for some reason I feel sorry for you. As a business professional, you are still bothering things that do not belong to you. It just hit me that you do not love yourself, so you couldn't possibly care for anyone else."

After a long pause, Natasha replied, "For what it is worth, I am sorry. Those words couldn't possibly cover the amount of damage I have caused, but I am truly sorry. My father is dying, and he decided to tell me and my mother now that he has another family. He told us this yesterday, and today I am at the home of two brothers and a woman I didn't know existed. I never held myself accountable for the things I have done because after having my childhood taken away by strangers who my mother was sleeping with, I found it better not to feel. Nineteen years of hurt, anger, and neglect have poured out of me in one day. Out of my family and friends, you are the first person to whom I have ever voiced that I have been raped. This is not for sympathy, but just to say now I got it, and I am truly sorry." Natasha felt a weight lifted from her heart and just saying the secret aloud, after holding it for most of her life, brought liberty. Ashley's response took Natasha's breath away.

"God forgives, and I forgive you too."

Chapter Thirteen

Everyone gathered around the dining table for an eight-o'clock breakfast, which was definitely out of the norm for Natasha. Tessa, dancing around the kitchen preparing things like the magic chef, seemed to be in her element. By the time everyone was seated, there was a spread of bacon or turkey bacon, scrambled eggs, grits, pancakes, and grape fruit with a variety of juices to wash it down. Michelle just looked at the table and let out a long sigh. Natasha placed her hand on her back and said, "Ma, you have to eat something." When Michelle examined the faces of unfamiliar persons and saw Bryant's resemblance in his sons and then looking at Tessa, she became furious. She began saying, "I can't believe this went on for years, and no one said anything. There wasn't an utterance of any kind speaking of what was going on. Bryant, we have had trouble in our marriage, I know! Is this the payback for my wrongdoing? I confessed my infidelity with the gardener and his crew, the wild nights, hell *all* of it. If my calculations serve me correct, these boys were walking and talking fully aware, and you said nothing to me. I poured out my heart about the loneliness and marrying you for money that was your opportunity to hit me with your best shot. *This* exceeds my sin hands down—"

Natasha interrupted Michelle's rant with news for the entire table, looking her mother directly into her eyes and saying, "Your sin didn't just hurt your marriage. I was caught in your escapades because you never checked to make sure your nightly rendezvous men were actually gone when you were finished. The second time your gardener paid a visit with his friends, I was sleeping in my room, which is in the other wing of the house. They had no business in my room, nor did they have any right stealing my childhood. I hated you for not listening when I tried to tell you what happened. You thought it was normal, and I had reached the flower of my age. Every time I heard men in the house after dark, I would hide in the laundry elevator until morning. I hid snacks in there because the visits became more frequent. You cared for no one but yourself!" Natasha placed her face into her hands and unleashed the tears she was holding back until she finished speaking. The room was silent enough to hear Bryant's teeth grinding together in fury. No one said a word. The food for breakfast went untouched after Natasha removed herself from the table and escaped into the sunroom. Michelle wanted to run after her, but her feet felt as if they were in lead boots. Her lips parted, but there weren't any words to follow.

Chapter Fourteen

It was three twenty-six when Natasha checked her cell phone hoping the past events were a nightmare, and not her life. Reality sunk in when her eyes came into focus, and she discovered she was in Nathanel's room. She grabbed her phone and dialed her home phone to see if Janet would answer. Natasha was desperately hoping Janet would be her perky self and be understanding and attentive as she always was when she told her of the latest happenings. Disappointed, she got her machine. Natasha started talking to the machine. "Hello, hello, chica, do not hang up. I am here, hola," said Janet as if she had just run a marathon. Janet continued saying, "You know it would've been great if you had called to let me know if ya had made it there safely. So how are the Hamptons?"

"Terrible," mumbled Natasha.

"It cannot be that bad mingling with the upper class. You fit right in." Laughed Janet.

"Well, before we left the hospital, my father informed me he had another family, and apparently he had told my mother the night before. She tried to kill him with Viagra."

"Wwhhhaaatttt?"

"Yes, I am at the Hamptons' at my father's mistress's house. I have two younger brothers, Bryant Jr. and Nathanel."

Janet replied at the pitch of a whisper, "Two brothers?"

"Yes, Janet, two brothers. The elder my father can't deny, and the younger one looks like a mix between Dad and his mother."

"Darn, you thought you were going to have to bury your father, not end up in the twilight zone," said Janet in a sarcastic tone.

"It is full of drama . . . ," Natasha hesitated in revealing everything to Janet. She had kept her secret so long that it became a part of who she was, but she knew it was time to let go. If she could tell Ashley Brooke of all people *first*, she could tell one of her best friends. "Also," she proceeded, "I had to tell my family I was molested by my mother's lovers."

There was a brief silence before Janet replied, "You had abuse written all over you by the way you acted. I guess this was a day of revelation to put things on the table in case something happens, no one will be left in the dark. Mamacita, I love you, and God told me I had to be patient with you, and you would come around. He wasn't lying, and He never does."

"He talks to you too?"

"Only when I am quiet enough to listen. When we get off the phone, I am going to call my manager, and let him know I need about a month off. I think you need me, huh?"

Natasha let out a sigh of relief and said, "You know me too well, but I have more drama."

"Jesus, Mary, mother of God, what else could there be?"

Natasha braced herself, then said, "The reason you didn't hear from me last night because I had an urge to call Jeffrey first. I called his house phone and Ashley, Bruce's assistant, picked up."

"Who's Jeffrey?"

Forgetting she never had the chance to talk to Janet about him, she briefly explained, "The guy I am interested in, but we will go into details later. Anyway . . ."

"Are they messing around or something?" accused Janet.

"No, he told me that was his cousin . . ."

"Uh hum," Janet interrupted.

"Anyway, she let me know she was the fiancée of the guy I slept with in college."

"You mean she was the pregnant chick who was preparing for the rehearsal dinner with the stuff in the front seat? I knew I had seen her somewhere, and her persona wasn't right when I visited you at your job that time, but assistants are known to be crazy."

The guilt in Natasha resurfaced from last night as she said, "She lost the baby due to stress, and she had to go to therapy the whole nine. We had a brief heart-to-heart after she told me how she wanted to take my life. Can you believe she told me she forgave me?"

"She must have found God in therapy because I didn't talk to you for two months after you told me that, and I didn't even know you like I do now!" exclaimed Janet.

Natasha wasn't fully aware of the changes being made in her, but Janet could tell there was something going on that only time could reveal. The ladies disconnected after Janet made hilarious small talk of the instances that occurred in her absence. Natasha called Dry Greens and gave her the same spill she gave Janet moments before. Landry told Natasha she would go and get Janet, so she wouldn't just sit there and worry. "I love you" is what Landry always told Natasha before hanging up the phone. She got used to the brush-off and the sound of the dial tone, but today Landry had to fight back tears because "I love you too" were the words she heard in reply from her favorite cousin.

All talked out, Natasha decided she would save Felicia for after dinner when she knew she was comfortable and not yelling at the DOW. Natasha darted across the hallway, which was luminous from the sunlight shining in from all the bedroom doors being open and the curtains pulled back, into the bathroom to wash her face. She patted her face dry and looked directly into the mirror at an image she had never seen. Her face was full of emotion, not the stern look or sly grin that peered back, but the look of a person who was actually beaten down with feelings. Natasha had never been the person to wear her feelings on her sleeves. Like a fortress locked and bound was the heart of Natasha, but this woman staring back at her is unfamiliar. The redness around her eyes along with the baggage gave her the unction to take a jog. She figured she needed to get active to think things through. Natasha changed and darted down the stairs. Her mother saw her go past the door and asked, "Where you goin', child?" Natasha yelled back in reply, "A much-needed breather!"

Natasha didn't consider herself athletic, but she was impressed that she never lost her stride. The winding road became narrower as she went in the opposite direction they came in from the airport. Cars blew their horns as they approached and passed as if to let her know they were there, and she was visible. She reflects on the week's happenings: "Monday, I quit my job, I refurnished my home, Janet came in from being on tour, my father in the hospital, found out about unknown brothers and their mother. Tuesday, I met the unknown brothers and their mother and found out Ashley Brooke was the fiancé." "Whooo!" is all there was left to say as the thought was complete. The thoughts continued, "Today is Wednesday, and I was supposed to go to *church* with Jeffrey. He never got back on the phone, so I could cancel. Since he knows the history with his cousin and me, I doubt he would want to see me again. Church may not be that bad at this point because the way my life is going, I will end up in hell." As she continued to ponder on if there was a heaven or a hell and that it may be *the* God, who keeps whispering in her ear, she started thinking about the direction she would want her life to go. Her secret was out, and she decided never to sleep with unavailable men who were available, so a change must come, *but what else*, she thought. It was a good thing the road was a dead end. Otherwise Natasha might have run a triathlon. As she drew closer to the house, Natasha decided she would get to know her brothers and their mother to see what would come of their relationship since she was tied to the boys by blood, and their only link together had a limited time on this earth.

When Natasha entered the house, the smell of garlic and seasoning inhabited the atmosphere and brought hunger pains to her immediate attention. When she made the sharp left to go upstairs to Nathanel's room, she almost had a collision with Bryant Jr. "Sorry, brother," she said and continued past him. He watched her head up the stairs with a smirk on his face and the feeling that they would finally loosen up, or *she* would rather. She reached Nathanel's room to find him standing there, painting next to the window in the corner. Natasha was wondering what was behind that sheet that towered in the corner and cast a spooky shadow in the midnight hour.

"Oh, hey," said Nathanel surprised to see her. "I have to finish this picture for a private auction tomorrow at seven."

"This is *your* room. I'm just visiting," said Natasha in a perky voice. "Do you always auction your paintings?" she continued as she gathered some clothes from her suitcase.

"No, I've painted as hobby since I was twelve, but as you can see it didn't stop there. I have a master's in fine arts, and so far I have painted for museums, politicians, and family portraits for the wealthy. It pays the bills and makes sense to me. What do you do and I am asking like I don't already know?"

"I was the head of marketing at Peagles, but I quit on Monday. You are the first to know in this house. I was all about the money, but now since that is no longer the object of my affection I guess I will have to find what makes sense to me," said Natasha staring out of the window without a clue of what that could be.

"When you find it, you will know, and you will be most happy," replied Nathanel while doing rigorous brush stokes to the canvas.

The scene played out just as it did at breakfast hours prior. The table is set, and Tessa is the last one to take her seat. Bryant Jr. took the initiative to bless the food, "Dear Lord, bless this family, and all that pertains to us. Father, help us to become unified and see each other as we *are* and help us to deal with things we cannot change. Bless the food so that it may be our strength in your Son Jesus's name, Amen." Everyone said in unison, "Amen."

The noise coming form the table was the clanking of dishes until everyone gathered what delectables they wanted. Tessa was in the mood for Italian when she prepared the shrimp and broccoli Alfredo or the option of pasta meatballs with the Cesar or American salads and garlic bread. The boys including Bryant knew whatever Tessa was in the mood for, Tessa cooked and didn't ask anyone else their opinion. Bryant opened the conversation by asking, "Natasha, how was your run?" She replied, "Good, I had so much on my mind that I ran out of road."

"I know I shocked you and your mother with my secret, and you have done likewise today, but for what it's worth, I want to apologize for my selfishness and for not being a better father, husband, and just better all around. The reason for my coming out is not to turn your lives upside down but to let you know what will take place when I pass on. Michelle and Tessa you will both receive twenty-five million dollars. Natasha, Bryant Jr., and Nathanel, you will be in full control of the company because I have your name on the largest amount of shares. You do not have to necessarily work at the company. There are people in place that I trust who will take care of things, but just be the eyes overlooking the operations. There is a Will, but since this is a gathering with everyone for the first time, I figured I should tell you so that there will be no surprises and unfamiliar faces," informing Bryant.

There was a brief period of silence. Everyone was in a state of awe because it was really real. Bryant was dying and there was nothing anyone could do to change the situation. The silence became too much for Natasha, so she decided to lie on the table her most current event saying, "Well, Dad, I am glad you parted the Will the way you did because I quit my job Monday and redecorated my home. I will be fine, but it is good to know that even though you weren't always there physically, you have always seemed to make sure I was okay."

"If everyone is up for it, I would like for you to come to my exhibit tomorrow. It is semiformal attire and starts at seven," said Nathanel, completely changing the subject. He added, "Dad, you didn't always approve of my career choice. You wanted me to be a businessman like Jr. and yourself, but this is what makes me happy, and I just want you to see how it makes others happy as well."

Bryant looked around the table and said, "Okay, we take a vote. All in favor of going to Nathanel's exhibit say, 'I' at this time."

Everyone agreed, and the night's conversation was out of the movies. The new family laughed, shared, and got to know one another on a more personal level. Natasha and Bryant Jr. found they had a love for sports and business. Michelle and Tessa had a niche for cooking. They exchanged recipe ideas and went back down memory lane with each ingredient from their childhood. In the midst of the conversation, Bryant leaned to Nathanel, who was sitting at his right and said, "I never disapproved of your career choice, I was just afraid you wouldn't be able to support yourself, and you just end up disappointed like my father did."

"You were a disappointment?"

"Yeah, I didn't have a career choice when he was alive, just doing odd jobs to make ends meet. I was twenty-seven when I found my career choice, and it made me happy."

There was so much laughter in the Hampton home one could mistake the address from days prior. The boys gathered in the kitchen to wash the dishes. Bryant gave everyone their specific duty, and they started work. There was loud conversation on past memories, basketball games, and women. The ladies retreat to the sunroom with tea in hand and Tessa with a book. Tessa sat in the chair aside the door while Natasha and Michelle sat in the loveseat. Natasha turned facing Michelle with her back against the armrest. She tucked her legs under her, sipped her tea, and watched the sunset. Thoughts of Jeffrey danced through her mind. She couldn't help but smile with the memory of their dance and the embrace they shared after the fashion show.

Tessa's voice rang in her ears interrupting her daydream, "Smiles like L-O-V-E."

Michelle gave a look of surprise staring back and forth and said, "Love? Who's in love . . . Natasha?"

Natasha let out a deep sigh and replied, "Well, with my past catching up to me, things could be ruined. There is no way I can fix it."

"Baby, this is not my department because I only fell in love with your father much later. I was in love with his wallet first. If it is the real thing, he won't let you go," Michelle bluntly replied.

Tessa exhaled and asked, "Could I put my two cents in?"

Natasha and Michelle looked at Tessa with smiles on their faces, and Michelle said, "You part of this family, shoot."

Tessa closed her book using her index finger to hold her place, removed her glasses, and began saying, "When you find that one true love, the connection is almost cosmic and can take your breath away. I found it hard to breathe when making eye contact with that person. My face would become flushed, and my hands would sweat. I always looked like a klutz when in his presence. He won't be able to turn his back on you if the feeling was mutual. By now, he is chasing you to see what your interests are and your circle of friends. Yep, he wants to be with you as well."

"How do you know?" Natasha asked Tessa curiously.

"I could tell by your smile when I said 'he's finding out your interest,' that that is exactly what he's doing. He really likes you. Just make sure he is not married with a child."

"By the looks of my rap sheet, I am done with married men. Speaking of the men, are they always that loud?"

"Yes, and it gets louder during any professional sports season. Mainly basketball and football, but they would get in an uproar over a family game of volleyball," Tessa said, followed with a chuckle.

Michelle looked through the glass door with a blank stare on her face and said, "He always wanted a boy. I got my tubs tied after you with no desire of having other children. I would have to be dumb and crazy not to notice that the two of you are in love. I say that to say, Nat, if you find the one, do not let him go. Material things will not make you happy. They wear, tear, and fade away to nothing, leaving you with nothing."

Chapter Fifteen

A sense of peace fell upon Natasha as she fell asleep. The calm of the atmosphere led her to believe that this sleep was much-needed. Her thoughts became louder in her mind, thanking God that she finally had peace with her mother and seeing her father happy in spite of his fading health. No sooner did her thoughts come across her mind than a small still voice whispered, "He's with me. Weeping may endure for a night, but My joy comes in the morning." A deep sleep fell upon Natasha, and she fell fast asleep.

Chapel music filled the temple with a sweet melody that made the corners of one's mouth turn up, no matter what their mood. Natasha found herself in a chapel entrance when the large mahogany door opened unto her. People were standing and smiling watching her as she entered. A veil covered her face as she walked, and yellow tulips were in her hands. There was a very delicate beadwork on her white gown with light washed yellow beading and pearls, which made her illuminate. Midway down the aisle, she realized she was getting married. At the altar awaited Janet, Felicia, Ashley, and Landry as her maid of honor. Her attention darted directly to the second pew with the sight of Oscar, who smiled and nodded with acknowledgment of her presence. Michelle and Tessa, both in tears, occupied the first pew. A million butterflies danced in her stomach as she got up the nerve to see who awaited her at the altar. Her brothers stood right of the groom, along with two other gentlemen she did not recognize. Her cheeks became tighter as her smile widened when her eyes met Jeffrey's. He looked like a dream in his tailored suit. It took everything in her not to run and jump on him with the multiplying amount of excitement. She kept her composure until she made it to the altar. Jeffrey removed her veil and peered into her with eyes that burned with such passion that it made her knees weak. Suddenly, there was an outburst of sobbing. As the minister was speaking, it got more intense to the point that everyone turned to see what the problem was. The ushers sped to Tessa's side, but her cries became more uncontrollable. Michelle was crying as well but tried to comfort Tessa, who was too distorted to stand. Natasha remembered what the voice said as she fell asleep and realized those sobs belonged to Tessa. Immediately, she got to her feet and ran to the commotion.

*   *   *

In her apartment with the television blasting, Natasha stared out of the window with anger mounting in her heart. The entire family became famous with stories about Bryant's affairs and other accusations. When she turned to everyone, she found their faces plastered to the television. On her new sofa sat Nathanel, J. R., Tessa, Landry, and Janet. There was an insert that proclaimed, "Like Father, like Daughter," speaking of Natasha's affairs with married men, one being her boss, and two others she hadn't seen or heard from in months. There was also some false allegation of names and faces she has never seen or heard. Everything that could dishonor a family was on every local station in the metro area. Natasha's phone rang to the point that Landry unplugged the landline and turned off her cell phone. A buzz interrupted everyone's concentration. Landry stomped to the intercom and rudely asked, "What?" The doorman announced, "There is an Ashley Brooke here to see you." Landry looked at Natasha's face with surprise. Natasha nodded her approval and Landry said with disbelief, "Send her up." Moments went by when a rumbling noise from the hallway sounded as if it were getting closer. When it got to the point of being unbearable, there was a sudden silence, then a knock at the door. JR got up to get the door since the men were put on duty to guard. He opened the door and laughed seeing that Ashley had her hand up about to knock again. "What? I took too long for you," JR said jokingly. Ashley laughed and sighed, saying, "This stuff is heavy, and the hop didn't help me with anything!" Nathanel jumped up to help and invited her in. A crystal vase of yellow roses in hand, Ashley asked looking at Natasha as she entered, "Where should I sit these?" Natasha snapped out of her unbelief and answered, "Just bring them in here," replied Natasha. Landry took them and placed them on the coffee table because unlike the other arrangements that were just mailed over, these were a delight to the eye. *Long stem with no thorns,* Landry thought to herself, *Someone cares.*

Ashley walked toward Natasha and spoke to the other members of the family as she went by with open arms ready to receive Natasha in her bosom. Natasha didn't know how to react. Ashley's petite body was almost half the size of Natasha's, but that didn't stop the embrace. It shocked Natasha that there was nothing fake about her hug. She received hugs from businessmen and women, even people from her own family, but never like this. There was compassion, and Natasha felt as if she would burst into tears if Ashley kept her grasp. Natasha wrapped her arms around her and hugged her back unleashing the flood of grief, hurt, and insecurities that kept her from truly opening up to others. The rest of the family looked on in amazement. Landry turned off the television and sat next to Janet placing her hand in hers. The boys did the same for Tessa wiping the tears from their own eyes. Moments passed before the wailing ceased. Natasha looked into the eyes of Ashley and smiled saying, "Who you are makes this impossible to believe. I have hurt you in the worst possible way, and yet here you are in my home allowing me to snot up your beautiful silk Chanel blouse. Not only that, but you brought food from my cousin's restaurant, which is enough to feed the nations, and you did it alone. Why?"

Ashley looked her in the eye and said, "Forgiveness is a crazy thing. When you get a chance to let something go that has eaten away at you and that has basically had you a slave to it for so long, you can't forget the person who allowed you to vent how you feel. I was angry with you for bursting what appeared to be "my" perfect world, which wasn't so perfect, but it was mine. Things happen for a reason, and who are we to interfere with the will of God? I feel a lifetime lighter. You could have been a butthole and cursed me, but you listened and accepted responsibility for your actions. You are a great person now that I have gotten over my issues to see that. When you forgive and let it go, you open doors to millions of possibilities. It is what you put out there, positive or negative. All of the NYC sees what you have put out there, but that person isn't who I see standing in front of me. Otherwise, I wouldn't jack up my Jimmy's dragging a pallet of Nerge for five blocks. God accepts us for who we are crud, mud, and all. If you are ready for Him your life will only be multiplied my Him. The God in me saw you needed a friend, so . . . here I am. Not to say I thought you didn't have any."

Wiping the tears from her eyes Natasha said, "Thank you, but God couldn't possibly want me. I have done too much . . ." Ashley interrupted before she could complete her sentence and asked, "Do you want God?" Natasha looked around the room with confusion and uncertainty on her face and answered, "I don't know. The only thing I knew I wanted in life was to have my own money and not to depend on someone else to provide for me, and to be in power. In all honesty, all I wanted was for someone to love me for who I am." Ashley informed, "God is love. He gave His only Son Jesus, the Christ, so that we could call upon Him because by Jesus is the way we get to God. Jesus on the cross suffered and died so that we could have life and life more abundantly. Accepting Him in this life gives us a guarantee in the next life, which is an eternity in heaven. There are no sorrows or tears, only joy and happiness. Not that Al Green stuff, but that real love and happiness only God can give. Do you know what I am saying?"

Natasha still had her doubts. A million thoughts ran through her mind. "Would this be the right time to ask about the small voice, how I know God really accepts me if I were to accept Him. Would I have to be a nun? Would I have to go to church every Sunday and Wednesday . . ." Getting a hold on her thoughts, she said to herself.

"How do I know God has accepted me? I am broken in so many ways. I can't possibly be fixed overnight, can I?"

Ashley smiled and replied, "Nothing happens overnight. We are not Jesus, but He is the example we strive to be like. As we embark on that journey, God takes away what will hold us back from our full potential." Ashley reached into her Louis Vuitton purse and pulled out a New Testament Bible. "I keep a mini Bible in my purse, read it and if you have any questions, just ask."

To their surprise when they turned to face the rest of the family, they had their faces in plates of Nerge and all you could hear was the clanking sound of forks to plates. It relieved Natasha to see Michelle had emerged from her room and joined the rest of the family at the table. Unlike the previous days, her hair was intact with makeup on and a rested glow upon her face. This is the family, J. R., Nathanel, Tessa, Mom, Landry, Janet, and the new comer Ashley. Natasha couldn't help but think, *Who would have thought that this could function but so far it is functioning. There are only two people missing. Felicia called from Tokyo and is headed back to the States as fast as she could get here. One other that never left her thoughts, and is a quiet echo in her mind at all times, is Jeffrey.* Natasha thought that it was not fair to ask, but as she and Ashley walked toward the dining area, Ashley turned to her and said, "Oh, the vase flowers are from my cousin. He sends his condolences." Natasha looked back at the arrangement and noticed that there was not a little card that was two-sided where people just sign and be on their way. There was an envelope that looked a little bulky, and on the outside, it read, "Read when ready, Jeff."

Chapter Sixteen

Bryant did a splendid job with the funeral arrangements. He made it, so everything was done to his liking and so that Michelle wouldn't have to put any thought into anything. His personal assistant and his lawyer carried out his wishes exactly as he intended. As the family stood around the open grave at Montefiore Cemetery, they could see flashing from news cameras and hear the dialog of reporters. The muggy weather made it difficult not to feel as heavy as the atmosphere above. Natasha looked over at JR, and she could see the frustration boil over in his face. He stormed off and headed right for the cluster of reports and onlookers. When he reached them, they proceeded to bombard him with questions asking, "Are you one of the sons or one of Natasha's lovers?" Then another asked, "Did Bryant split the fortune equally between all of the children even though two were illegitimate?"

JR's voice sounded like the eruption of a volcano when he commanded, "If you are not a member of this family, whether functioning or not, get the hell away from us so that we can bury Bryant Billingsworth in peace. Haven't you any respect for yourselves? Haven't you any shame?" JR turned and walked away fixing his tie and thank God, he hired as much security as he did. A misty rain began to fall on the small mob as JR took his place next to his mother. Nathanel stood left of Natasha with his hand around her shoulder and her right hand gripping his. Melvin stood on her right comforting Michelle who couldn't stop sobbing. Landry, Felicia, Janet, and Ashley stood behind the family as if to form a burier between all that wasn't near, dear, and personal to their world. "Ashes to ashes and dust to dust, may you rest in peace Bryant Billingsworth in the name of the Father, the Son, and the Holy ghost," announced the minister.

The small mob started to deplete moments later, giving their condolences and their regrets. Some of the faces were familiar and others weren't. Bryant's friends offered to do any handiwork necessary and gave their cards to Michelle while they needed no introduction to Tessa because they were acquainted with her and her sons. A moment like that would unnerve most women, but Michelle was relieved she didn't have to go into any extra explanations while she fought back tears to greet and thank those who came. The minister, suits, and other gatherers had departed leaving the family there at the site. The workers stood by so that they could shovel in the dirt, and the funeral home directors stood a short distance away, being sensitive to the families' need to say good-bye. Natasha broke the silence by saying, "Mom, do you remember when Dad would come home from a long trip and always bring what he would call footprints of the places he had been. Horseshoes from Texas, tokens from Vegas, you know, so I could imagine that I had gone with him." Michelle shook her head as she wiped the tears and said, "No, sugar, I do not recall." Tessa began to tear up and said, "I won big on the slots when we went to Vegas and he kept tokens to remember the great time we had. He also took me and the boys to Texas something like a 'family vacation.' That is when he and I decided to tell the boys the reason of him always leaving. The boys wouldn't speak to him for months when he came to visit, but after a while, they accepted the situation. I just wish you guys could have been included sooner. Unlike an episode of Jerry Springer, we actually get along realistically. I know this is a messy situation, but the choices you make affect everyone and everything you do, and you are forced to sleep with it when the bed is made."

The family threw in their long stemmed red roses after going down memory lane and sharing a few laughs. Natasha took a second look at them and realized this is what she needed in her life, people to be real with her and not pretend that everyday is a great day and that everything will be peaches and cream. Her friends and Landry had been her mirror for years, but it is great to have an unexpected new addition. As Natasha walked lagging behind the family, her mind became very quiet, and everything became still. She knew that the small still voice was coming, and she anticipated the words it would speak. Then breaking the silence, God said, "I Am the great I Am, The giver and the taker of life, and the author and the finisher of everything. Ashley is one of my servants, and the information she gave about Me and My Son Jesus is true. I wouldn't visit you if I did not want you, and I never say anything that does not stand true. I whisper to you to teach you, to inform you, and to guide you. Accepting My Son and Me fully into your heart and into your life will wash away all the wrongs you have done. I have a sea called "Forgetfulness" that all sin is thrown into upon the acceptance of My Son. Read what she has given you and ask what you will. I know you totally, now I want you to know Me."

Natasha was the last to get into the limo with her family. She placed her leg into the vehicle and her right hand on the door frame to brace herself for one look back. Her head turned but not before a stream of tears rolled down her cheeks. *Father is gone. There is no bringing him back,* she thought. There was a figure she noticed on the hill past the site with the silhouette of a man just standing there watching her as she watched him. There was no camera in his hand or any thing that gave indication that he was taking note. It made Natasha uneasy but not as unsettled and his gesture. He raised his hand as if it were a gun and drew it back as if he had just pulled the trigger.

Chapter Seventeen

The buzzer on the wall set the butterflies in Natasha's stomach in disarray. It had been two weeks since her father's death, but it felt like an eternity since she had seen Jeffrey. He sent her flowers everyday since she received the first bouquet. She had yet to get up the nerve to read each letter but had made a home for them on her bedside table and placed a red ribbon around the nine letters. He was on his way up to take her on their first date. First, to bible study. The rest of the evenings activities was left up to Natasha. Natasha felt obligated since she had agreed to it weeks ago. The buzzer sound once again, and Natasha ran to it forgetting she didn't answer it the first time.

"Hello," she said into the intercom.

"Ms. Billingsworth, there is a Jeffrey Pattman here to see you," informed the doorman.

Natasha's breath became short and shallow with excitement and nervousness. She composed herself and said, "Send him up." It came back to her remembrance that she hadn't gone on a "date date" since she was fifteen. "We're going to church for crying out loud! I need to stop talking to myself." A knock at the door interrupted her conversation. Natasha looked through the peephole and saw the face that she longed to touch since they last danced. She couldn't help but smile with the memory of their embrace. His attire consisted of a fitted button down vertical strip dress shirt. She noticed his sleeves were rolled up from him raising his hand to knock again. Natasha quickly grabbed the door handle and flung the door open before his hand made contact. Jeffrey stood at the entrance a few moments with his hands still raised captivated by

Natasha's beauty. Natasha began to blush and asked, "Will you come in?" There was still no response from Jeffrey, so Natasha said his name "Jeff," and stated, "You're making all the blood rush to my cheeks. Please stop looking at me, and come in." Natasha moved to the right behind the door with her right arm extended. While her hand was still extended, Jeffrey crossed the threshold and took Natasha in his arms. He whispered in her ear, "Natasha, how I missed you!" She locked her arms around his neck and held him as tight as she could. In response, Jeffrey said, "You hug me like the feeling is mutual." They inhaled each other's scents and for a moment were enslaved to their longing for each other. Jeffrey loosed the firm hold his arms made around Natasha's frame where there were a few centimeters of space between them. In turn, she let her hands rest on his hips. Jeffrey gazed at Natasha with passion in his eyes and a single thought in his mind, *I wish I could love her and show her without making a fool of myself.* Natasha had her eyes closed afraid that this was only a dream and opening her eyes would only reveal that he is not there, and this is another daydream. Jeffrey whispered to Natasha, "Open your eyes." He caressingly placed his hands on her cheeks and positioned her face to his so that when she opened her eyes, she would look directly into his eyes. Her knees became weak, and her hands clammy. She braced herself before she let him into her completely. Natasha knew with lovers in the past not to ever get so close, so personal. Jeffrey wasn't someone from her past. She wanted him to be in her future and every aspect of it. She exhaled gently and opened her eyes. Natasha felt as if he could see into her soul. Her heart burned within her chest when she realized the rhythm their hearts made. She held on to his wrists to keep her balance as she thought, *I wonder does he think as highly of me as I do of him. God if only this moment could last the rest of my life . . .* Interrupting her thoughts, Jeffrey asked in a whisper, "Can I kiss you?" She swallowed hard. Her mind was racing screaming "yes" in reaction to his question. Natasha closed her eyes and lifted her chin with her lips parted ready to receive his. She was surprised at how soft his thumbs were as they caressed her cheeks. Jeffrey received her invitation closing the gap between their lips. They found themselves engulfed once again in the same passionate embrace without the ability to let go. They lost themselves in each other without hopes of being found.

Natasha looked surprised when they entered the residential neighborhood of the middle class. The new surrounding caught Natasha off guard reminiscing on their embrace only eighteen minutes before she left the car ride silent. She blushed like a teenager when Jeffrey looked over with satisfaction knowing their thoughts were in sync.

They began to slow up as they approached the last house on the street. It was well lit and a two-story stucco beauty with large windows which had shades drawn open showing the living area where people were sitting around obviously having a great time. Jeffrey announced, "We're here. I hope you weren't expecting a church. Bible study is held in rotation at different ministers' homes. I figured you wouldn't feel too uncomfortable since this is Ashley's house." Natasha just smiled and nodded. Jeffrey said, "Okay," as he removed the keys from the ignition and proceeded to Natasha's side and opened the door. As Natasha looked through the windows, she felt at ease with her attire being MEK Jeans and a Karen Kane wrap shirt seeing other women in tees and jeans—very casual ensembles. The walkway was lit with mini bamboo lights leading you to the front door. Jeffrey grabbed Natasha's hand and looked her in the eyes for assurance that she hadn't changed her mind. Knowing what he was doing, she jokingly said, "Don't tell me we are really crashing a party." Giving a giggle, she nodded in approval. He knocked and moments later, a tall dark and handsome man opened the door with a big smile on his face. "Hey, I thought you forgot where we live," said Dreek embracing his cousin as if he'd been away for months. "You are the last ones to arrive. I'm going to introduce myself, I am Dreek Brooke, and it is great to hear you and my wife have become great friends, my condolences for your loss and double that for the drama. We're all family here. Come in and make yourself at home," he continued with a gesture to enter. They entered and Natasha gave the place the once-over. Seven feet in front of the entrance, there was a stairway that led upstairs which split going either left or right. She looked to the left of the stairway and saw a dining area with a table that sat eight with wine and crackers on the white linen cloth table. Her scope was interrupted by Ashley saying, "Hey girl," giving her a hug and continued saying, "Let me introduce you." They walked to the right and turned into the living room where everyone was socializing on an extremely long cherry leather sectional with disposable cups in hand. Ashley got everyone's attention with two claps and saying, "Everyone, attention, this is Natasha." Everyone said in unison, "Hello Natasha." Natasha waved and smiled. Ashley replied, "You did not have to sound like we are in an AA meeting. I'm going to start to the left. Next to my husband Dreek are Kevin Wriggly and his wife Joanna." The three were posted by the oak coffee table while the others continued to talk on the sofa. "Here you have starting on your left are Steven and his wife Mika, and you already know Jeffrey," Ashley said with a giggle.

As Natasha approached the sofa to sit next to Jeffrey, she noticed a dark figure outside the living room window. She gasped trying to find her breath and tried to focus her eyes to see if she recognized the person. Jeffrey turned to look out the window to see what brought on her reaction. He saw nothing and looked back at Natasha. "What is it?" he asked with his brows creating creases in his forehead. Natasha looked at him with surprise as if breaking out of a trance and trying to remember where she was. She answered, "There was some . . ." she broke off when she looked out of the window and saw no one there, "I guess it was nothing," she completed. Dreek and Jeffrey went outside to scan the property just in case.

Ten minutes passed, and Dreek brought everyone into focus so that he could open the Bible study in prayer. Everyone stood together and held hands with their heads bowed and Dreek prayed saying, "Dear Lord, let us be transformed by the hearing of your word, let things learned land on fertile ground and be written on the tablets of our hearts, in the name of Jesus." Then he proceeded with the lesson informing Natasha by saying, "We have studied forgiveness for the past three studies, Natasha. If you like, Jeff can give you the notes, so you can read over them," Natasha looked bashful and said, "Okay," as she stared at her Bibleless hand wondering why the subject kept entering her life. Dreek's voice became background noise when thoughts of her life and what people have done to her came into view. There was a new battle in her heart now, which was forgiving herself for all she had done. Although the example given brought her back into the room as Dreek spoke saying, "In scripture, the harlot, who had many sins to forgive, used her tears and hair to wash Jesus's feet. She enraged people because they felt she was not worthy to even touch the Son of God. They were upset because Jesus allowed her to do so. The acts we do to gain God's forgiveness may by frowned upon by those who are looking on. Those who are close to you will see the transformation. They may be patient or they may turn against you, but those who love you will stick close in those times."

The lesson for Natasha hit very close to home. She couldn't help but wonder if they saw the news when her father died about her exploits, but her curiosity overturned other emotions that were battling inside her. Natasha raised her hand feeling out of place and yet in the right place and asked, "Dreek, do you have to make your asking for forgiveness as public as this woman?"

"No," Dreek said with a smile and continued, "You can seek forgiveness in the privacy of personal prayer. If there was something to be forgiven between you and another person, you can simply go to that person."

"What if that person does not believe you are sincere?" inquired Natasha.

"That person must take it up with their God. Forgiveness is for the person who is asking for it. Whether it is returned is the receivers' option."

"It sounds easy to ask, but is it really that easy in God's eyes?"

"It is that easy if you truly mean it from your heart and let it go, yes that easy."

There was a brief silence after Natasha's questioning, then Dreek asked if there were any more questions. Silence continued, so Dreek took it as a "yes" and proceeded to ask, "Does anyone want prayer?" The silence lingered again, so Dreek took it as a "no" and did a closing prayer to dismiss the study.

The good-byes went in a breath's time to Natasha. Before Natasha knew it, she was standing next to Jeff waiting for him to open her door. He used his best moves in opening the door pretending to be her driver. She blushed when he turned to her hand extended and smiling. She got in looking at him as he proceeded around the vehicle. Natasha reached over and opened the door for Jeffrey, then made herself comfortable. He turned the key in the ignition, pulled a u-turn in the street, looked at her, and then asked, "So what do you think?"

"Think about what?" Natasha asked looking confused.

"The study; you looked like you were there, but not."

They had come to a four-way stop and Natasha could feel his eyes on her. She wasn't sure how to feel with her inner battle and all of the emotions she had encountered lately.

"It was good, but Jeff, I am not a believer. Tonight I am taking it into consideration. I just have things internally I'm dealing with along with everything else, and I am not feeling 100 percent comfortable talking to you on a dark street at a four-way."

He laughed when he realized the truth in her last statement and asked, "Have you decided what we are doing? This is your half of our date."

"Let's bowl," Natasha said with excitement like the activity had just arrived in her mind, which it did.

Chapter Eighteen

Natasha overlooked her shoulder to the man of her dreams and couldn't help but smile. He gave her the lane as a courtesy, bragging that he would win regardless. She was so excited to find a lime-green bowling ball, awaiting her arrival. *Loser,* she thought as she took the ball as a sign. The night's curiosity had her full of questions. She had not bowled since high school and felt her making a fool of herself would take the edge off the questions she wanted to ask. She threw the ball down the lane and turned to ask her questions before it made contact.

"Do you follow God like Dreek," she asked.

Strike

"I guess you're a pro at this," Jeffrey asked in amazement, then focusing on what she asked. He then replied, "No, I have my own walk with God. No one has the same calling; therefore their walk with God is a little different."

Above on the monitor were animated features that acted out each turn with exaggerations like an old comic book. Jeffrey held his head high as he took his place and the top of the lane. He inhaled deep and then rolled the ball. Contact was made but only three pins went down. "I will be thoroughly embarrassed if you beat me. Maybe this one will be better. Why do you ask?"

"All of my friends believe in God and I don't, but lately I'm starting to change my mind. You are the first man I have met that expresses knowledge of the unseen being." Jeffrey only knocks down three other pins in reaction. Natasha says sarcastically, "Maybe I shouldn't talk until we are done."

"No, you're fine. I just suck tonight. It is your beauty, not my game," he replies laughing at his own corny line. Natasha grabbed her ball and then took her place at the lane. She threw the ball down, then turned asking, "Do you hear voices? Not bad things, but a soothing voice"

Jeffrey looked surprised for two reasons; one, she rolled another strike and two, he was taken aback.

"How do you keep rolling strikes?" Jeffrey stood, putting his arms around Natasha and saying, "No, I personally do not hear voices, but my mother could hear voices, or the voice of God. She said it was calm and still. God helped her raise me since my father died when I was three. I, on the other hand, have dreams that tend to come true with very little differences in the dream versus the reality." He looked back at the lane, then at the score and asked, "Would you like me to take you home before you put me to more shame? It's getting late."

Natasha looked up at Jeffrey and asked, "Will you say you got beaten by one rusty Natasha Billingsworth?"

"Of course."

*   *   *

Jeffrey and Natasha came to a halt in the lobby of her building. He grabbed her hand to stop her from proceeding to the elevator. She looked surprised, but knowingly, Jeffrey would stop and draw the line here. He kissed her hand asked her to call him when she made it in and locked the door. She nod in agreement, smiled, and then headed for the elevator. Natasha took her last look for the night and entered the elevator. This was a first, she had gone to Bible study, and a date proceeded thereafter. Second, they didn't even sleep together. Last, but not least, she somehow fell in love with him. Natasha could feel the blood rush to her cheeks when she thought on his smile and couldn't wait until she saw him again.

Chapter Nineteen

It is quiet when Natasha entered her apartment. There were no more family members occupying her space. Janet and Nathanel got very cozy before she had to leave to finish her South American tour. Natasha didn't feel it robbery that Janet wanted Nathanel to see her off. "Maybe she and Janet would be sisters after all," she said aloud laughing to herself. She laughed to because she got comfortable that she had an extension to her family. "Shoot! Jeffrey."

On the way home, Natasha programmed his number on speed dial, and she was glad she did.

"I started to turn around thinking you were stuck on the elevator," said Jeffrey without a proper greeting. This made Natasha warm inside to see he truly cared.

"I am all in. I had a great time."

"Me too! If it is okay, can I call you tomorrow?"

"Course," she replied, smiling, anxious with anticipation.

"Tomorrow then. Goodnight, Tash."

"Night."

As soon as she closed the cell phone and kicked her shoes off as she entered her bedroom, there was a throbbing pain to the back of her head. Natasha couldn't help feeling dizzy and falling to her knees. She pulled her hand away from the back of her head, no blood. When she turned around, there was an intense pain across her cheek. Out of reflex, Natasha pulled her hand to her face and made an attempt to crawl away from the unseen assailant. As she crawled away, she was kicked repeatedly. In pain with the feeling that all her internal organs were in her throat, Natasha became frustrated. She turned on her back to find herself staring down the barrel of a gun of a masked man. She didn't know whether to be afraid, or unleash the adrenaline that was building.

Breaking the stare down with her attacker, he asked, "Are you prepared to meet your Maker?" Natasha was surprised because the voice of her attacker sounded so familiar.

"I am asking the questions! You give a yes or no answer. Ms. Billingsworth, are you ready to die? I can place *my* worth on you going to hell."

Natasha took her time answering the question. She grabbed her stomach because after several kicks, there was a ripping sensation in her lower abdomen. If these are her last breaths, she figured she would make the best of it. Living for God in eternity can't be nothing short of bliss. If, and only if she survived this, she would live for Him for the rest of her life on earth. A feeling came over Natasha that she grew more excited to feel. Even more than knowing Jeffrey was close and this feeling had intensified and became a longing. There came her favorite voice, calm, peaceful, still saying, "Ask how you get ready to meet your Maker?"

Natasha slid her pain-filled body toward her bedside table to lean against it. Her attacker thought it an attempt to get away and kicked her in the stomach again. "You can't get away from me!!! You had your family at the funeral and your boyfriend tonight, but I know you'd be alone tonight, except me of course."

The voice spoke again saying, "Peace be still. Turn over to see his eyes, then ask, 'How do you get ready to meet your maker?'"

Natasha did as she was told and locking eyes with her assailant, she felt a familiarity in the eyes. Swallowing this feeling, she asked, "How do I get ready to meet the Maker?"

The question took her attacker by surprise. The gun was lowered and then the masked head tilted to the side. After moments which felt like an eternity to Natasha, who started to spit blood, a reply came asking, "Are you asking me the road to salvation? I have lived to see everything. This whore is asking of me the road to redemption. The lives you've wrecked! You broke homes, marriages, and damaged the lives of children. If only you could have kept your slutty legs from around my father, our family would be okay. *You* caused this, and you ask for life!!! I made it in my mind that I would end your life and that is just what I have come to do. What you do for eternity is up to God." The masked man knelt closer to her, then asked, "Are you ready for the return of the Lord? Answer honestly."

Natasha began to cry because she realized she wasn't ready, but if she had to meet God to take the pain away, then so be it.

"Answer me!"

"No, I'm not ready," Natasha answered through her sobbing.

"Repeat after me, Father."

"Father."

"I am a sinner."

"I am a sinner," Natasha repeated.

"I have seen the error of my ways."

"I have seen the error of my ways."

"Please forgive me."

"Please forgive me," Natasha repeated.

"I accept your Son Jesus Christ into my heart."

"I accept Jesus Christ into my heart."

"To be my Shepherd forever and ever," said her attacker.

"To be my Shepherd forever and ever," she repeated.

"Amen," finished her attacker. He stood upright and aimed the gun right at her face. There was a loud noise that made the attacker turn around. When he did, Natasha found the strength to slide closer to the bedside table and grab the revolver out of the drawer. Turning back around, Natasha was dizzy. She closed her eyes and pulled the trigger. The last thing Natasha could breathe was, "Jesus."

Chapter Twenty

The sweetest melody you can hear is the music of heaven. Living water flowing though the city where lights illuminate so bright you can hardly see. The music like a river of voices singing, "Worthy is the Lamb that was slain." Instruments of a million strings playing heavenly, unlike anything heard before on earth. Bliss and peace is the only way to describe the feeling. A still small voice came to Natasha saying, "Not yet, daughter, not yet."

Natasha woke to more familiar voices. They did not possess the same level of peace and comfort, but they made her happy. Her mother was talking to Janet, who was close to her, speaking in Spanish.

"You have been on that phone since ya got here. I do not want my daughter waking up from a coma speaking Spanish. Nathanel, tell her to get off tha phone right *now*."

"Mrs. Billingsworth Natasha is used to me speaking Spanish. If anything, she will wake telling me to shut up. I have to make sure they cancel all my shows. Thank God, it was a short tour. Otherwise, Nathanel would have to take care of me," replied Janet.

"Okay, you two," Michel said to break their embrace, "Nathanel your mother and brother are going to take shift in a few minutes, so let's prepare to clear out. We have to check on Jeffrey. He is still critical from the gunshot. Ashley cleaned Nat's place for me, and I need to tell her, "Thank you." Get off that phone, and come on here!"

Natasha could hear movement, but she realized no one knew she was awake. She felt trapped, and everything felt heavy. Natasha could have a breakdown internally, and no one would be able to detect. A nurse entered the room and checked her status. She must have been thinking out loud when she said, "I am sorry this happened to you, honey. Your baby is alive and well in you in spite of your three broken ribs and punctured lung. They will take time to heal. We are working hard to keep Jeffrey alive. We know you didn't mean to shoot him, but he is getting better though he still has his good days and his bad days. Now, all we can do is wait, and make sure everything heals properly. The rest of the family is on the way up to switch shifts. I keep telling you all these things so that you won't be totally left out when you wake up."

Suddenly, a warm feeling came over Natasha's entire body. It was like fire was shut up in her bones. The only thing Natasha could do in reaction to this comforting heat was shouting, "Jesus!" The machines around her started making noises, and she could hear the still small voice say, "He whom the Son sets free is free, indeed."

The nurse was startled and dropped everything in her hand. She yelled down the hall for the doctor and extra help. Natasha could hear the clacking of stilettos, which sound like a herd of buffaloes. Her family doubled back when they heard the nurse shout, and they beat the staff to the room. The nurse used her body to hold them off.

Dr. Milton arrived and asked, "Let me through please. It is critical that I see her before you can enter."

To Be Continued . . .

Edwards Brothers,Inc!
Thorofare, NJ 08086
06 August, 2010
BA2010218